It started as a roar, like the sound of water rushing through a canyon in a flash flood — distant, unrelated, ominous, but unidentifiable.

And then they appeared. Running, four abreast, the red-uniformed Visitor soldiers rounded the corner of Main and Third, thundering down the street toward the courthouse.

There was still enough of a crowd to mobilize some resistance. A few braver ones ran toward the soldiers trying to block their passage. Perhaps those few thought they would be killed for their efforts, but they were not. No shots were fired. The people stared open-mouthed and their movements became random and chaotic. Somewhere someone was screaming, but no one in the street screamed.

And then the Visitors climbed the steps of the courthouse and the old stone building swallowed them up. As quickly as it has begun, the invasion was complete. And once again there were no red-uniformed lizardmen on the streets. Now they were everywhere. And none were visible.

THE OREGON INVASION

Look for these *V* titles from **Tor Books**

V
V: THE OREGON INVASION

Jayne Tannehill

THE OREGON INVASION

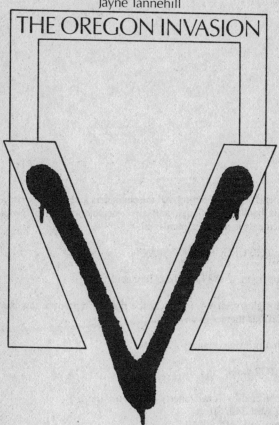

A TOM DOHERTY ASSOCIATES BOOK

V: THE OREGON INVASION

Copyright © 1987 by Jayne Tannehill

First printing: January 1988

A TOR Book

Published by Tom Doherty Associates, Inc.
49 West 24th Street
New York, NY 10010

ISBN: 0-812-55729-8
Can. No.: 0-812-55730-1

Printed in the United States of America

0   9   8   7   6   5   4   3   2   1

To John,
who had the dream;
and
to Bill,
who traveled the path with me

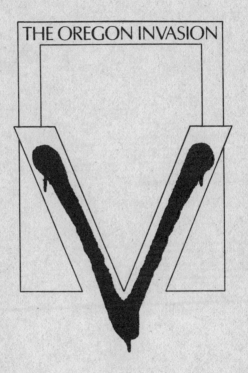

THE OREGON INVASION

Again he raced down the endless white corridor, around the corners, past slamming doors, down the stair tower, out into the open, away from the building, away from the computer voice announcing the closing, pressing presence of death, away from the pressurized air ducts forcing the death into his body, out into the desert, alone, racing alone, all alone, no one else escaped, alone, running alone, pursued by the red-and-gold balloon, alone, beyond its grasp, beyond the wind, running alone, all alone, unable to run, all alone, overtaken and surrounded by the red-and-gold balloon, pouring red dust slowly over his body, over his head, over his body, over his hands, over his head, over his head.

Hadad woke unable to scream.

The dream again. The dream he had never lived. The dream that seemed more real than life. He shook himself free of the images.

The desert was dark and still. Below him in the valley, the last lights of Prineville outlined the farms and streets. A few cars twisted down the far hillside toward the city. His pulse shuddered and began to calm again. He pushed on the ground beneath him, forcing his body up and down to release the adrenaline pumping into his muscles, making them tighten in spasms.

It was only a dream.

He hadn't had that dream for months. At first, when the news had first come of the red dust, the defeat of his people, the departure of the mother ships, then he had understood the dream. Then he had wakened each time certain that the red dust had reached Prineville. And each time he had waited for the dust, for the death to follow, and nothing had happened. That was over a year ago.

The Visitors had come to Earth on a directive from The Leader. Earth was selected because of its water. The Visitors were to take the water, collect protein-based life forms for food to be preserved and brought home—home to an overpopulated, starving world.

The sentient beings of Earth were easy to conquer, awed by technology, eager to believe they were valued by those smarter and more powerful than themselves.

But later there was resistance. For when reporter Mike Donovan got aboard the mother ship over Los Angeles and discovered the Visitors were not human, as they appeared, but lizard beings disguised as humans, it took no time at all for the xenophobia to spread. That, coupled with the revelation that the Visitors were collecting humans for their food-storage compartments, changed the tenor of the invasion. No longer could the lizard Visitors count on the unsuspecting hospitality of Earth.

The invasion had become a war, and Hadad was not a warrior. For months he had continued at his post aboard the mother ship, regulating the cryogenics compartments by computer, checking the life-support levels as thousands of food packets arrived from the planet and filled the holds. For months he had avoided the war.

But Diana had discovered an error—one body that had warmed suddenly and breathed its entire oxygen supply and then died; one body she had wanted to restore to life. And so she had removed him from his post and sent him to Earth as one of Stephen's assistants.

Hadad had accepted the demotion without argument. Before, she had taken his authority; now she had stripped him of rank. Gradually he realized that she watched him for any failing, any shortcoming, jealous of the favor he had from The Leader.

But that was behind him. That was over a year ago.

He hadn't meant to be left behind.

He had just grown so hungry for the deserts of home. The Leader had said they would find Earth was just like home. It wasn't. There was nothing here like home. Except the desert. He had only meant to escape for a few days into the desert. But his English was so bad. He wasn't supposed to go to Los Angeles. The ship that hovered over Los Angeles had been organized for the Fertile Crescent. He was to organize the party to the plains below the Dead Sea. Even his name suited him for the plan. And then Diana had objected to the plans. And their ship had gone to Los Angeles.

He had been lonely.

His departure from the compound had worked too well.

The stolen clothes had been easy. He had started to walk, but his boots were not suited to the streets of Beverly Hills. He had sat on a curb to rest and the gardener had offered him a ride. Asked where he was going.

He had tried to say desert.

He wasn't certain what he had said or what the man answered. All he knew was the man wanted to give him a ride. And so he had ridden, uncertain where the man would take him. Uncertain how to find the desert he was looking for.

In two days he had ridden in five trucks, learned from one man how to hold his hand to stop another truck, to get yet another ride. Everyone had asked where he was going. After a while he had just pointed down the road.

Once a man had asked his name. That he had

understood. But when he had told the man "Hadad," the man had screamed at him to get out of his truck. Hadad wasn't certain what a "damn foreigner" was. He never told anyone his name after that. He had used David's name instead.

His pulse returned to normal and he stopped the pushups that were almost second nature. Earth ones had watched him do them once and been amazed at how many times he could repeat them. He did not understand their amazement. But he had learned not to do them when there were Earth ones around.

He had not meant to be left behind.

Sometimes in the middle of the night, when the night creatures had finished their nocturnal scavenges for food, when the lights of the city had been turned out except for the outlines of the streets and the floodlights on the courthouse, he had dreamed about going home on the ships. Above all, he wanted to go home.

He'd been at the rodeo when the news came that the ships had come back. It hadn't taken him long to figure it out. If they could have gone home, they would have. There was no reason to come back to Earth. It was death to his people to be here, to be anywhere near the red dust. He waited for death himself. It was only time, he figured, time for the poison to reach his own food supply. It never occurred to him that Prineville was not in the path of the dust-carrying winds. It never occurred to him that he had found, accidentally, the only place he could have survived. Until this evening.

And then the dream had returned.

He shook himself free of its returning influence.

Fear made him hungry.

The night creatures were stilled around him. They had fed earlier. He crept out of the cave he had made for himself just below the shelf of the plateau above the fairgrounds. From the cave he could see most of the town. He could watch the sun rise over the forest to the east. He could survey the grasslands to the north. And no one knew he was there.

Quietly he walked down the hillside, walking with his senses alert to any sound that would betray some wakened creature. There was nothing. Nothing stirred until he reached Coombs Flat Road. A car swung around the corner from the fairgrounds on the way to the reservoir. He recognized Chuck Martin's car, and waved as the headlights caught him on the road.

Chuck waved back.

When Hadad had left Los Angeles, he hadn't aimed for Prineville. He had pointed down the road. The road had brought him to Prineville. The only decision he had to make was when to stop. He might have stopped a few miles sooner if he'd been awake. But he had fallen asleep somewhere in the mountain roads beside the great white mountain, and when he woke, the driver had stopped for gas in Prineville.

It was desert. And so Hadad had stopped and headed out into the hills, up to the plateau that jutted into the town, level with all the plateau lands that surrounded it. Some places there were fenced grazing lands, other places were open. No one saw him in the hills.

For a while he'd been content hiding, living in the rhythm of the high desert animals, feeding as he found food, avoiding the howling creatures he'd later learned to call coyote. His first encounter with the coyote was on his own territory. The coyote had seen him sitting by his cave. It had approached him by smell. And then suddenly it had stopped, wary of the lizard that looked like a man, wearing men's clothing. They had watched each other all night. And in the morning they had both watched a field mouse, neither willing to yield the prey to the other, yet afraid to leave their guardedness, their watchfulness of each other. He had learned the coyote's patterns. The coyote had learned his. They sought the same food. The coyote had yielded a portion of the territory. Enough. But in time the sparseness of the area itself had driven Hadad into town.

At Third Street the logs were stacked waiting the teeth of the sawmill. There were always mice among the piles of logs. One night he had moved too quickly and started the logs rolling down the pile out into the parking lot. The night watchman had shot toward him. The bullet had torn his artificial ear, but had not touched his head. The next time, he had not tried to climb the stacks, content to scout the dark sides of the bottom logs, always assured of enough to eat.

He had been seen.

A few nights later the night watchman had seen him again. This time he offered him food instead of shooting him. Hadad had accepted the sandwich, but he didn't eat it. The night watchman had talked. When he realized Hadad didn't know English, he talked louder. But he still talked. He called himself Dave.

And so Hadad called him Dave too.

Dave had suggested he get a job at the mill. Hadad didn't know lumber. He did know computers. He did know electronics. He did not know lumber. But he could sweep. And so he did. And he could carry things. And so he did. And he was stronger than a man his size would have been, and so he carried more than most. And that way he had gotten money. And then he could go into town.

English wasn't hard to learn. They called him Arab at work. He wasn't sure what that meant. At first it sounded like "damn foreigner" had sounded. But after a while it sounded like Dave or even like Hadad, though no one knew his name was Hadad. They thought his name was David. They had asked for a last name. Hadad had thought they wanted the name he had had before and so he said Hadad. And so they had called him Mr. Hadad. But no one called him Hadad. They called him Dave.

He laughed now at how foolish he had felt trying to work with so little knowledge of English. On the ship he had spoken his own language. He had never seen Earth ones, not live ones. Only the packaged ones stored in the hold. He had monitored and repaired the computer-controlled refrigeration tanks. He had been in charge. He had not needed English.

He stopped at the night watchman's shed and shared a cigarette, a few words, and then he went out to the stacks and stacks of drying logs. A tap on the right log brought a mouse to the surface and he grabbed it and popped it into his mouth. He picked up three mice and a small lizard before he came back around to the shed again. He hadn't liked lizard meat on his own planet. The little ones on Earth were sweet.

"Heading home?" the night watchman asked.

"Yes. I think that will be enough until morning."

"You shore do like your walking. Never knew a man could get so much outa just walking around in the dead of night. Me, they have to pay me to do it. Maybe you should be the night watchman."

"No thanks, Dave. That is your job."

"That's true, Dave. I sure couldn't do the heavy lifting you do all day, not with my old back. 'Night now."

"Good night."

Hadad walked back up the road toward the fairgrounds, on toward the hill that was home. He had learned this town. No one knew him. But no one suspected him of anything. He had appeared out of nowhere, needing work. When they asked where he came from, he had said Pau. That was the city he was to build below the Dead Sea. It was the only city name he knew that was not in an English-speaking part of the world. Someone asked him if he was Hawaiian.

But he wasn't sure what being Hawaiian would mean and so he shook his head. Then he'd pointed down the highway, the way he'd come. And someone had asked if he came from California. He had said Los Angeles. And that was all that was needed. It didn't even matter anymore that he didn't speak English. People just shouted at him. And gradually he'd learned the words and they had stopped shouting.

He had not meant to be left behind on Earth.

He had only wanted to spend a few days in the desert.

He had seen the maps on the computers.

Gradually he had accepted that he could not go back to the ships. The news from the returned ships filled the programs on the television set in the bar at the fairgrounds. He had watched along with the cowboys who had come to town for the rodeo. They had watched as Diana had been kidnapped. They had all seen how she had been protected from the dust. And later he had heard that the Visitors were back and were safe as long as they stayed in the open cities. And then the news had become distant. The Visitors were not in Central Oregon. They might have taken over Southern California. They might have taken over all the major cities of the world. They were not in Central Oregon. And therefore it didn't matter.

Given a few beers on a Saturday night, the fellows at the bar might have a few suggestions for the rest of the world on how to get rid of their unwanted red-uniformed invaders. Most of the men in town carried weapons, and thought the rest of the population should as well. It took Hadad a few hearings not to tense when he heard the familiar: "Why, if one of them was to walk in here, I'd shoot first and ask questions later."

They didn't mean they would shoot him. He wasn't a Visitor. Not anymore. For a while he had been "a drifter." That sounded like being a "damn foreigner." Then he'd been "the kid out in the hills." That didn't sound like "damn foreigner."

He had needed something called an address. It was numbers and names. That he knew. And so he had looked for a number and a name that would go together. He had chosen 1047 Deer. Someone had said, "Oh, you live out by the railroad tracks." He didn't understand. He had learned what a deer was, and that did not help him understand why the man had said he lived by the railroad tracks. But the numbers and name satisfied everyone who asked. He never bothered to find out what an address was supposed to do for a person. One day he had not found food and gone to work late. Someone said they had been around to his house looking for him. That was the only time anyone looked for him.

He climbed the hill now behind the fairgrounds. He was tired and the nightmare had been put aside. When he reached his cave, he circled, checking to be sure he was not observed. And then he settled inside, curling into sleep, facing out into the world as an animal does that does not trust.

"Gclixtchp?" His mother called from the house.

He ignored her first call. His attention was focused on the thin wires he was tracing over the circuit board.

"Gclixtchp?" This time she called in that insistent tone that meant a lecture would follow. He made the soldered connection and turned off the circuit maker. He was drawing in copper. Later he would copy the pattern. For now it would wait.

"Gclixtchp! If you don't learn to come when you are called, someday you are going to be left behind!" She threw parcels at him that must be taken to the transporter. She expected him to go with her. There was no arguing.

The familiar glottals and fricatives exploded in his ears. "If you don't learn to come when you are called, someday you are going to be left behind." Somewhere the conscious mind registered the anachronism: His mother did not know English and the words were clearly English. He knew . . . what did he know? Corridors of white replaced the sands of home. Long channels of bodies, this one starting to decay, must be removed. Check the seals, why was it rotting, who was responsible?

"Incompetent!" Diana's voice shouted and echoed down the corridors.

"Incompetent!" Her eyes fired their disgust at him. He had dared to complain about her orders. Now he was a necessary nuisance, no longer an organizer, no longer a leader, only a broom-pusher, button-pusher, "incompetent."

He had never pushed a broom on the mother ship. That anachronism woke him. He shook off the dream.

A coyote howled. Another answered. Something flew past his cave. It was still dark. He closed his eyes. The lenses burned against his lids. He would get liquid in town in the morning. He could not risk leaving his lenses out until his lids could rest. He reached for the bottle of liquid above his head, hoping there would be a little left. His hand missed the bottle and caught on the root pressing down into his cave from the juniper growing above.

"Damn foreigner," he cursed the darkness. His artificial skin, his "plastic," was torn. Now he must find the "medicine plant" that would glue it back together. They were plentiful in the stores in Los Angeles. He had had trouble finding them in Oregon. And they did not grow in the high desert, not naturally. He had tried to grow one by his cave. It had survived the summer days, but the cold of winter had killed it. He would look for one in the morning, squeeze the flower-leaves until the white liquid oozed from it that would stick to everything, especially his "plastic."

Dave had taught him that word. . . . "'Plastic,' that'll open all the doors, let you go anywhere, buy anything. All you need is plastic." He was right. This was all Hadad needed: plastic. Without it he would be shot. It did not matter that he was working, doing the job no one wanted to do. It did not matter that he ate only the rodents that the farmers tried so hard to get rid of. It did not matter that he knew the cowboys, cheered their victories, laughed at their stories, drank their beer. Without the plastic he would be shot.

He bandaged his hand, making sure the pink met under the bandage so that the green beneath would not show dark under the wrapping.

He found the bottle of liquid and tried to squeeze the last few drops into his eyes.

It was less painful then to close his eyes. But that did not make sleep any easier. If he had heard the Earth ones' superstition that in the moment before one dies one's life flashes before one's eyes, then he would have known he would soon face death. But he did not know that folktale and so he watched the drama mixed together with fantasy and fear. In the night the coyotes howled, the desert was restless, and so was he. He tossed, unwilling to give up sleep, unwilling to give up to sleep.

And then it was dawn.

He had dreamed of going home and knew he could not. He was committed to Earth as a prisoner condemned to an island jail, having full freedom of his territory, but not of his life.

He had dreamed of going home.

And there, over the forest to the east, just beyond the ridge of the far plateau, there in the morning blush, haloed by the first gold of daylight, there in the too-blue morning sky hung the mother ship.

Chapter 2

Hadad stared at the disk in the sky. Part of him wanted it to be there to rescue him, to take him home. But that did not fit his notion that they could not go home. And they would never have sent a ship for *him*. And no one knew where he was; they couldn't have traced him this far north. Logic told him the ship was there as the ships had been everywhere, to launch yet another invasion.

It was not that Hadad was particularly concerned for the plight of the people of Prineville. They were polite to him, gave him work, accepted him on the fringe of the community. But it wasn't that he really cared whether or not they maintained their pioneer determinism, their small-town spirit, their control over the county, over their corner of the world. If his people took control as they had elsewhere, then it was only because of some superior force or numbers or organization. He had never questioned the concept that might makes right. He had been recruited, taken from home, because that was the will of The Leader. He had been diverted from his role as a commander by the will of logic, Diana's logic! That was the way of events. Power was a product of political influence. He accepted that. And power in the hands of those he knew frightened him. Not because of Prineville, but because the food balance was so precise in the desert. There would not be enough small rodents to feed the ship. The larger predators would be eaten. And then the desert would be overrun with rodents and the crops would begin to die, and then the small animals. The land was already showing the signs of depletion.

Junipers dotted the plateaus. Prineville was not being invaded; Hadad's territory was being invaded, and he was afraid.

He reached behind his rocks to find clean clothes. The night's tossings had ground the desert soil into the ones he wore. He changed quickly, noticing that the bandage he had put on his hand in the night had come loose. He replaced it, able to see now that the rip was more serious than he had thought. He worked the bandage round and round, giving the appearance of a severe wound, but covering the unmistakable green beneath.

The morning was sharp and clear. He had learned that on mornings like this Earth ones wore jackets. He put on a jacket and took the folded leather container that held his earned money. He tried to remember the name of the leather package, but the word "wallet" would not come to him.

He needed a medicine plant. He would go to Erickson's. It was easier to follow Crooked River down to Deer Street into town than to trace the neat squares of streets and houses, and so he followed the gulley down to the river, crossed the park, and avoided civilization until he had reached the western end of town. In taking that route he avoided seeing the groups gathering at the fairgrounds, at the county high school, at the courthouse. His first encounter was with the shoppers at Erickson's.

There is a feel to a supermarket at 10:30 on a Wednesday morning. The shelves have been re-stocked; the carts are almost all in the store instead of scattered around the parking lot; there may be a few ladies in line, an older man, no kids, a trucker, perhaps, getting a pack of cigarettes, but none of the usual menfolk.

It was not a usual Wednesday morning.

Erickson's was crowded. Lines formed at the three open checkouts, and the manager was filling a fourth register to open himself.

"No, we aren't closing at noon."

"There aren't any tomatoes."

"*They've* gotten them already."

"But they don't eat tomatoes."

"That's beside the point. You eat tomatoes. What good would it be for them to take only the things *they* eat? The idea is to starve us out."

"No, I can't leave the checkout to help you, Mrs. Grundy."

"Better board up the place, Pete, they'll be here in no time. Better board it up. I've got an extra rifle. We can stand them off."

"I wouldn't let the children go to school this morning. I've got to get home."

"Shirley, I have the same problem. It's not going to get you out of here any sooner pushing past everyone."

"I have to get home. My children are alone."

"They set one foot in this town and we'll let them know they can't take over a decent town like Prineville."

Everyone talked at once. Acquaintances who had only nodded to one another for years compared strategies for protecting the children, barricading doors, stockpiling arms.

Hadad walked into the chaos and in an instant the store was silent. He looked from one face to the next as the fifty people or more stopped their shopping to watch him. He buried his hand in his jacket pocket, afraid that his bandaging was not enough. He suddenly thought about the liquid for his lenses. His pulse accelerated. Body reflex stopped all extraneous muscle movement. He tried not to bolt.

"Oh, that's just Dave." The manager's recognition came in that next moment and the crowd moved back to their individual projects, the conversations muffled for a bit until the fear that he was one of the Visitors had subsided.

Hadad watchfully began his shopping. He passed women grabbing food and piling yet more into over-crowded baskets. He looked for some logic in their choices and found none that he could grasp. The shelves were sparse, looking like a late Saturday evening before a Sunday holiday. Everywhere there were spoken or whispered concerns: The teenaged girl would be raped, the county official would be replaced, the railroad that was the county's pride would be taken over, the children would be brainwashed, the farms would be turned into vermin-infested breeding grounds for rats, the produce from the valley would be cut off, the rodeo would be canceled, no one would come, the motels would go bankrupt. Every concern predicted the town's impotence to withstand the invasion; no hope of turning back the unwanted Visitors.

There were no sundries on the shelf. No drops for lenses, none for eyes. Hadad looked around for the few plants that sometimes stood near the checkouts. They had been replaced by special displays of choco-late and peanut-butter cookies.

He stood in the line, waiting to pass the inspector lady at the checkout who would ask him for his packages and let him pass because he had none.

"Don't you have no packages?"

"No, I couldn't find what I wanted."

"I know what you mean. Isn't it awful? It was like this when they had the truckers' strike a few years back. It's like a stock-market crash is on the banks, you know what I mean? People just can't see that everything will be all right if they just take things in stride. Always out for number one, you know what I mean? You don't have to stand in this line. Just go on through, over there, that's what I do when I don't find anything; yeah, over there by the carts, go ahead."

Hadad took the lady's advice and ducked under the bar that demarcated the cart racks. The manager looked up and smiled at him as he headed for the door.

The air outside was still. The ship hung over the hills, but there was no movement, no landing party, no military invasion, no armed resistance. A few cars moved through the streets, obeying the usual rules, pushing the limits in the usual ways.

Hadad headed up to Fourth. He would try the Posie Shop. Sometimes they had medicine plants there.

The flower shop was empty. He rang the little bell that always called someone from the back room, where they made up bouquets. No one was there. He went around behind the cash register and looked into the back room. No one. He looked outside, in the shops to either side. No one. He found the medicine plant that he wanted. It was a small one, but it would do. He could grind the sticky substance and get enough for his hand. That was all he needed. He would water it and keep it beside the cave. If it did not die, he would have it for later. He left the money on the cash register, carefully counting the bills and coins to be sure he had the correct change.

He still needed to find the liquid for his eyes. And then he must go to the lumberyard and tell them why he was late to work. He went back to Third and over to Bob's Market. He could always find what he needed there. And then he could go on down Third to the mill.

There was a group gathered around the counter at the front. Like the shoppers at Erickson's, they all stopped talking when he walked in. He felt the same pressure, the fear that he was the first attacker invading their refuge. He walked past the group and began a search in the back of the store, looking through the frozen foods, though there was nothing there he wanted or needed. He wanted time to let his pulse slow before he tried to find the little bottle, afraid his own fear would make him clumsy.

"Who is he?"

"Just a guy from down at the mill."

"He's all right."

"Don't worry about it."

"He's not . . ."

"Nah, they call him 'Arab.' Drifted into town months ago."

"You know him then."

"Trust me, I know him."

"There hasn't been a landing yet, that means we still have some time."

"I say we shoot first, ask questions later. Maggie says I'll get in trouble that way, but the way I see it, if we wait to find out what they plan to do, they will already have done it. They made all the promises before. They were here to destroy us. I say we destroy them first."

"Fine, but how?"

"We've got guns."

"And so do they."

"We need to get everyone together. They'll beat us with numbers as long as we're all strung out all over the county."

"But if we gather in town, who's gonna protect the ranches? I can just see it, we hole up in the courthouse and wait for them to surround us. What do we gain with that?"

"He's right. They clearly have the advantage. We don't know what they're gonna do."

"So what are we supposed to do, just wait?"

"It's better than spending all our energies fighting ghosts that never show up."

"But we have to be prepared."

"What are we preparing for?"

"Well, one thing we know, they're gonna come out

of that spaceship and take over. The only thing we can do is kill them before they kill us."

"That's for sure. You can't argue with those fascist techniques of theirs."

"Then we ought to surround 'em rather than let them surround us."

"How do you surround them; they're up in the air!"

"We have to let them start somethin' on land so we can get on 'em and strike *them* down."

"Fellas, you're not talking about some religious end-of-the-world freaks who think they are going to save us all for some great guru. You're talking about a trained army designed to take over the whole territory. They've done it before. We are small potatoes to them. Look, when they first came, they tried the peace and sugar-coating routine. We exposed that. So now they aren't hiding; they want to destroy the Earth and all of us with it. They'd rather eat us for breakfast than mess with us."

"You're wrong. We're useful to them somehow, or they would go away."

"We are food for their table, Clyde. That's all we are: food for their table."

"Look, something else must have happened. Something we don't know about yet. Something that hasn't been on the news. Why is the ship here? Why here? Crook County isn't big enough to interest a food-scouting party. We're all spread out. Why not pick a big city where they can find all the food they need?"

"They're after more than food; they're after control."

"It doesn't matter what they're after; we can't let them have it."

"But if you don't know what they're after, how can you keep them from getting it?"

"Look, we need a plan."

"We need people. Figure all of Madras, all of Redmond, all of Bend; then we might have a chance."

"How are you gonna get all those people to come up here and fight?"

"If they don't come *here* and fight, then they'll have those fascist redcoats in their backyards!"

"I'm not arguing with you about that. I want to know how you are gonna get them to come and help *us*."

"We've gotta call people. We still have the phones, haven't we?"

"As far as I know."

"And we need a centralized location—a place we can meet and find out what we need to do."

"Let's use Cary Fisher Hall. That's big enough at least."

"And we have to make some attempt to gather weapons. One shotgun by itself doesn't cut it against an army. We need to group whatever strength we have, plan how to use it."

"Most of my ammo is out at the ranch. A couple rounds and I'd be a gone goose."

"We have to assume they aren't afraid to die. That makes them harder to fight. You can't scare them."

"That's what I say, make every shot count."

"But the other thing is, we can't make it look like we're organized or they'll see how piddly our forces are. We have to fight underground, just like they report on the news. Strike when they're not looking."

"But the thing is, everything has to look normal on the surface or the whole operation looks suspicious. The kids have to be in school, the people have to be in their offices and shops, the banks have to open as usual. We can't declare a holiday. It has to look normal, at least as normal as possible."

"Why don't we just shoot the sons of bitches?"

"Because they can shoot back."

"I'd take out a dozen a' them before they could get me."

"But they'd still have got you, and you're more use

to us alive than dead."

"Hey, lady, you figuring to win this war without a few casualties, you're crazy. We're gonna die out there. That's what we're talking about. You can have your organization, all you want. You can beg people to come and help us, and they might be dumb enough to do it. But don't give me this 'better alive than dead' garbage. We have one chance in a million of coming out of this alive, no matter what we do. The only safe way out of this is to run away before they get some notion this place is inhabited."

"I haven't noticed you running, Joe."

It wasn't until Joe had identified the one voice as a lady that Hadad had realized she was. She was as tall as any man there; she wore boots, pants, a leather work jacket, and a cap like anyone down at the mill. He realized she had been the one suggesting organization. He watched, waiting for her to take over the way Diana would. She didn't. She added her ideas and stood her ground, but she wasn't in charge. Hadad was curious.

The market was long and narrow. Three aisles ran the length of the store toward the street. In the back, one little room contained all the freezer chests. He had chosen that space as refuge from the stares as he came in. Now the townspeople were absorbed in their planning and he was forgotten. He walked slowly up the far aisle, looking at the shelves, holding his plant under his arm, edging closer to the group so that he could hear more than the louder voices.

The front of the store was glass, and through it he could see across to the county courthouse set back behind the fountain. A group of men were gathered on the courthouse steps in an animated conversation. One man kept walking away and coming back. Another paced on the steps, first toward the group, then two steps away, then back with another suggestion or comment. The man below him on the ground pointed his finger up at him and waved it forcefully to accentuate every point he made.

Hadad found his eye drops and took them from the shelf. He had no intention of interrupting the conversation to get to the cash register, but he wanted an excuse to stand in the group. He was not yet confident that they would accept his being there. At some point he must leave, go to the mill.

And then he saw his boss at the mill, Mr. Ripley. The man crossed the street over to the courthouse, then crossed back to Bob's Market. He looked inside, then called to the men on the courthouse steps. They all came across the street and crowded in the door.

Now there were several conversations at once. Everyone had an idea, no one had a plan. Everyone had a solution, no one had a clear picture of the problem. Everyone had a point of view, no one had a concept of the forces or the issues they were about to fight.

Mr. Ripley quieted the group. He was used to large groups of men, used to giving orders and being heard. He was used to taking charge. He did what he was good at. It did not matter that his ideas were no more thought out than any others.

"Men, we haven't time to . . ."

"I don't get it. What's the big hurry?"

"Larry, shut up and let the man talk."

"No, you shut up. He's talking about going out there and getting killed, and he says there isn't time to consider that there might be an alternative. There isn't a man in here who's been in a war in the last twenty years. You gather your guns and play cowboy come springtime, shoot a few rabbits, maybe a deer during hunting season. But not one of you has killed a man."

"These aren't men."

"Maybe they aren't men. But they dress like men, and they walk like men, and they talk like men, and I even hear they breed like men. We are not talking about shooting some dumb animals that can't outreason us. We are talking about inviting well-trained soldiers to shoot at us by shooting first at them."

"So what's your big alternative, Larry? What would *you* have us do? What was your suggestion: that we all run off into the hills, just give up Prineville? Just walk away and let them have it? Maybe you haven't lived here long enough yet, boy. But I was born and raised here. This is my home and it was my daddy's home before me. That ranch of mine is all I have in this world, and no red-suited infiltrator is going to take it away from me whether he comes from this world or some other."

"What are you talking about, your ranch! Mike, all you have in this world is your skin! If you don't protect that, there isn't going to be any argument about any ranch."

"All right, all right, men. You both have a point. We need to take time to look at all the alternatives. But we also need to organize what forces we have. The mill is closed for the day. I sent some of the men up to Barr's, on the pretext of lunch, to see if they can get some of the people up there organized as well. The rest of the guys have gone home to get their families and what weapons they've got. Bob, I know you don't have any ammo on the shelves, but you know where to get it. The rest of you get your business taken care of and get your guns. We'll put a man in every store in town. If one of them comes in, shoot first and ask questions later."

"You do that and you'll all get killed. There won't be any town left to take over."

"Look, we don't even know why they are here."

"They've invaded every city in the world, do they need to explain any more than that?"

"Maybe they do. We're not a major city of the

world. Why are they here in the middle of Central Oregon? Maybe they just want to find an open space to live in and settle and raise families. Why are we assuming they have to be killed just because they are aliens? There is a lot of room in Central Oregon for people to live in and settle and be constructive."

"Oh, my God. Listen to the man. You'd think we hadn't already learned all about them. You've seen the papers, man. You've seen the television programs. They have taken captives; they have stolen water; they have killed anyone who stood in their way. They have no interest in peace. 'Maybe they want to move into Central Oregon and live and settle and be constructive.' Sure, they do. But they're gonna eliminate all the competition first. And we are the competition, man. We are the competition, and they will drive us out or kill us in the process."

"Wait a minute."

The girl in the leather jacket spoke again.

"We don't have to put ourselves in a paper bag and shoot our way out to prove we are the smarter inhabitants of this town. Mr. Ripley suggested we get what weapons we have. Even if we don't use them, that makes more sense than being unarmed."

"I don't go nowhere without my gun, lady."

"That's fine for you, but it's not true for all of us. Personally, I don't ever want to kill anything. I don't even eat meat."

"That's your problem."

"No, it's not my problem. It's the point of all this. We don't want to kill anyone, or we wouldn't be standing here arguing about it."

"Speak for yourself. I'd love to get a little target practice."

"Harv, you get plenty of target practice. And I'm not gonna let you shut me up with your macho line. Whatever we do to get organized, we can't move against a force that doesn't do anything. And we can't fight them unless they come down here and fight. So all this talk about guns is only part of it. We can't stay holed up in stores waiting forever. We have to go on living our lives. You can't keep your kids home every day. They'll go crazy. We have to go on living our lives. And we have to know where to go, what to do, how to organize if and when something happens."

"I vote for the fairgrounds. Everybody can get in there."

"And you're a sitting target for anyone up on the hill, let alone up in a hover craft."

"Better the hospital; we might need the supplies there."

"That's a point."

"So can we at least agree on that? If something happens, we all meet at the hospital?"

"Fair enough."

"I'm still for getting men in all the stores."

"Mr. Ripley, where do you draw the line? Which Visitors do you kill on sight? Which ones do you watch to be sure they don't do something wrong? And how do you define 'something wrong'? There have been resistance fighters on all the ships all over the world. I can't remember what they call them. How do you know you won't be killing one of them? They could help us if we knew who they were."

"I say we kill 'em. They're Visitors. They ain't one of us. There ain't no reason good enough to suit me for them to even be here."

That sort of ended the organized discussion. The last man to speak was the first to leave. The others stayed, seeking small audiences for the points they had not yet made. Mr. Ripley managed a few recruits for his plan to arm the stores of town, and sent a few men up to the café on Main Street to tell his other followers about the plan to meet at the hospital. A few people had actually come in to shop and they now turned their attention to the shelves, hunting for items necessary to whatever ordinariness they expected of the day.

The girl in the leather jacket had come to speak to the store owners, and now that the group was clearing, it was evident that she had a satchel between her feet. She lifted the bundle onto the counter and opened it.

"I think I picked a bad time, all around. I didn't know about . . . Oh, what the hell . . . we talked about you selling some of my pieces on consignment. We might as well forget it . . . but I brought some things in to show you. Do you want to look at them now?"

The man behind the counter nodded and spoke very quietly. Hadad couldn't hear his voice over the argument beside him, but he figured it was okay because the girl started taking out pieces of leatherwork and holding them up. It seemed strange that the girl was bringing them here. This was a market, not a clothing store. There were a few things—gloves, caps, socks, underwear, utility items—on the rack against the far wall, but no garments like these. The man took a jacket and tried it on. Perhaps he was buying for himself. Hadad wasn't sure.

He wanted to see the leather goods. He had never seen shirts like that. He had seen jackets. A lot of the men at the mill wore them. But he had never seen a shirt that looked like skin. And there were pants, men's pants that looked like the legs of a deer.

The garments were laid aside and from the satchel the girl pulled belts, pouches, watchbands, a woven strap, a lady's cap, a pair of gloves.

Hadad edged closer to the counter and reached out with his unbandaged hand to touch the gloves. The man and the girl stopped their conversation to acknowledge him, but he was not aware of their response. He was aware only of the softness of the glove and the tight, even stitching on each finger. The belt was not so soft, but the braiding baffled him. He could not see where the pieces could have, must have, couldn't have twisted, braided, woven over and under and back where they had started, not where they had started. He tried to trace one strand and lost it, tried again.

The girl laughed.

"That's a mystery braid. It's easy. I'll show you."

Hadad shook his head and turned away from the counter. It was enough that it was braided. He did not need the mystery part too. The girl and the man went back to their trading.

Mr. Ripley had said the mill was closed for the day. Hadad did not need to go and sweep or carry. He did not have to explain why he was not at work this morning. He did not have to show his hand. He did not have to go anywhere, and so he stayed in the store listening to the people, hearing their concerns. At times he had the urge to tell them the limit of the arsenals aboard the mother ship. Except for weapons that had been invented while they were on Earth, the ships were only limitedly armed for terran battles. That did not make them less dangerous. But the imaginations of the scattered Earth ones were far more elaborate than the munitions departments on the ships.

Hadad watched the patterns of fear. Each man who joined a cluster would assert first his authority ("They have no right to be here") and then his strength ("I'd kill every damn one of them before I'd let them near my home") and then his deepest concern. (Here there was more variety: For some it was a homestead, for others a child, for others an ailing wife, for a few their own lives.) Finally would come the confusion, the wavering between action and inaction. In time each would settle into a point of view: For some the only solution was to kill the aliens; for others the only solution was to run away; for a few there was resignation, a willingness to endure anything just to be allowed to believe nothing had changed; a few showed cunning—the watchfulness that does not move before the right moment, the planning that mentally calculates the alternatives and what is needed, gained, lost in each, silent impatience with the noise of confusion, guarded waiting that does not concede.

The cunning sifted through the crowds, waited while the unsure drifted out of the store, on to carry out or abandon their schemes for survival. The cunning waited, and when the last person who carried the smell of panic had left the building, the organized conversation began again. This time it was quiet, reasoned, purposeful.

Hadad began to measure the group. The girl was still there. He could not pin down her energy. Her words were those of a pacifist. She had already said in a dozen different ways she did not kill, as though there had been someone there trying to convince her to do so. And yet she carried a throwing knife. Hadad had seen the outline of the sheath between her shoulder blades as she stretched forward showing the shop owner the leather garments. She talked about passive resistance, but when an aggressive strategy was proposed by someone else, she had a suggestion that would improve it. She had the eyes of a deer, and the mettle of a fox.

The man called Larry stayed. Hadad judged his body as he would an opponent for a fight. His power was in his shoulders and arms. He could outswing Hadad in a moment. And his body was trim, no indulgences turning into complacency. He was alert but not strung tight like a man eager for battle. Hadad's reflexes would keep him out of the man's way in a scrap. The man was careful. Hadad concluded he would rather have him as an ally than as an opponent.

Three men had come in together. Hadad knew them from the mill. They didn't talk much. But Hadad had seen them at work. They did the job. They collected their pay. They didn't look for ways around the boss, or take extra coffee breaks. That much Hadad knew. He looked now at each of them. The graying man had a scar just below his right eye. The impulse was to look away if he looked at you, to stare at the intricacy of the stitched-together face if he looked away. Beside him stood a man who could have been his son. His body was armored with the same taut fibers. His face was empty of expression, but his eyes blazed with intensity. The third was shorter than the others. A wiry man who looked more like a dancer than a lumberman. His body was limber, his movements liquid. His power was in his legs and in something undefinable called presence.

One other woman had come into the store and stayed. She had come over from the courthouse. Her graying hair was taking the last signs of youth. Wrinkles and plumpness, arthritis and a bad back had taken their toll earlier. But there was determination in her stride and purpose in her words. And no one discounted her contributions.

A cockroach walked daringly across the front of the counter. Hadad watched him test the air and venture from behind the cash register toward the edge, over the electric cord, and down the front of the display case. Hadad became aware that he was hungry. He had not had breakfast. The few mice captured in the middle of the night no longer sustained him. Four men stood between him and the counter. As the cockroach descended the case, he watched, moving his head slowly from side to side to keep his prey in sight as the legs intervened. The roach stopped, moved back, turned, stopped again, turned back in the original direction, and moved forward. It stopped again and did not move.

Another pair of legs pushed into the space. Hadad felt the shoulder nudging him to the right and yielded.

The cockroach did not move.

"Either way, we can use the additional numbers." The girl in the leather jacket spoke and Hadad looked up, then back to the cockroach. He hadn't moved.

". . . I'd say they're power hungry."

"There are two ways to know you have power. One is by using it. The other is by not using it, and watching the resistance mobilize to defeat you. You can figure you have just a little less power than the opposition figures you have. So if you ever have to use it, you'd lose. The only way to win is to get the opposition to use its own power against itself."

The cockroach started moving again, this time across the case out of Hadad's range.

"They'd be smart then if they just stayed up there, didn't come out at all."

"How do you figure it?"

"They know we know they're there. If they come down right away, we've got two advantages: First, it's our territory. We have the knowledge of it, and we have the passion for it. Second, we're afraid. If they come down now, you saw what I saw. Ripley's gang isn't organized, but the fear's pumping so hard in those people that, given someone to focus on, they could tear a man limb from limb with their bare hands. But if the Visitors wait, even an hour or so, that initial shock is gonna wear off. And then every one of those cowboys is gonna be eatin' his own liver wondering what he's gonna have to do. I'll bet not a one of those guys will even think to stop for lunch, and come about four o'clock, their gullets are gonna betray 'em."

The cockroach reversed his course and the movement caught Hadad's attention. He watched as it came back across the case and started down toward the floor.

"Then you're saying what I said before. We ought to go on doing what we normally do. But we're still going to need more people."

"I'm not disagreeing. We can use all the help we can get. But we don't need another thousand people running around crying, 'The sky is falling, the sky is falling.'"

"I'm not suggesting that. But surely we each know some people we trust, some people we could call."

Hadad watched as the cockroach reached the floor. He wasn't certain in which direction it would head.

"Okay, that's one strategy. But what are we trying to accomplish here? We get lots of people, so what? What are we trying to do?"

"Kill off the Visitors."

"Why, Pete?"

"Why?"

"Yeah, why?"

"Carl, what do you mean, why?"

"That's the hard way. What do you want to kill them off for?"

"So they don't kill us off."

"That's my point. We don't have any reason to kill them off. They might have a reason to kill us off —we're in their way, we taste good—who knows? But we don't have any reason to kill them off. We don't gain a thing collecting dead lizards except a disposal problem. It's enough work to bury a cow when it dies. We don't need them dead. What we need is them gone."

"What are you gettin' at?"

"Look, if our purpose is to kill them off, we can do

that. Ripley is right, we arm the town, station the troops on the second story of every store on Main and Third, and draw the suckers down the path and shoot 'em dead. You can watch any 'B' western on the tube and learn how to do that. That's simple. But what do we end up with? A spaceship hanging over our heads with enough big guns to end the game. It's not the O. K. Corral, folks. I mean, in a situation like that, what do you get if you win? It seems to me we better know what it means to win in this game."

"I guess what it comes down to is who do we want to wake up with when the shooting's over."

"You got it."

"Well, I don't want to wake up with no perverts running Prineville."

"Pete, we're all a bunch of perverts. You've got your definition. I've got mine. Right now the only perverts I'm worried about are green lizards pretending they're humans and hanging up in that spaceship. When the shooting's over, I wanna know they're gone."

"So what do we do?"

"We have to make them uncomfortable here. Make it too hard to do the simplest things."

"That's passive resistance."

"There's nothing passive about it. Have you ever tried to physically hold a child who's trying to run away? Not punish him. Not force him to do something. Just hold him in one place. This is gonna be just like that. That's not passive. That takes every ounce of strength you have and every ounce of willpower too. Not to mention imagination. You have to second-guess 'em. Figure out what they want to do, and then figure out how to make it difficult. The only easy part about fighting that way is you don't have to do anything special to get ready for the fight. You just have to know what the fight is about and what it means to win."

"We still need to organize. We need to set up a headquarters or something."

"Look, what's wrong with right here? We're across the street from the courthouse. They're big for taking over the system. If they move in there, we'll be right under their noses. We can watch the whole thing right in front of us. We all got here this morning somehow. Why make it fancy? You okay with that, Bob?"

Hadad watched the manager consider the possibilities and the alternatives. He didn't say anything; then after a moment he closed his eyes and nodded.

The cockroach sensed the completion in the crowd and anticipated movement. His leisurely pace across the shoetops and traversing the open planes of floor now stopped. He froze, then turned from side to side. He would run in a moment, Hadad tried to calculate which way.

His best bet was to scoop him up with his left hand. If he ran to the right, he'd have to let him go. The foot beside the roach moved and the beastie shot to the left. In one movement Hadad scooped him from the floor.

No one had particularly noticed him before the movement. Now the attention was again on him as he straightened up, the cockroach palmed in his hand, trapped by a finger, still wiggling. Hadad looked up into the questioning eyes of a burly man with a heavy brown beard and hair as long as the growth on his chin. If he had known the mountains, he would have thought "bear," but Hadad had never been in the mountains. The man's eyes questioned what he was doing.

"Thought you dropped something." The words came garbled from his dry throat, his voice almost taking on the throaty vibratory resonance natural to his people that they had worked so hard to eliminate from their speech patterns to emulate the Earth ones.

He pretended a cough to distract the audience, explain without explaining.

The burly man shrugged and turned away. The cockroach wiggled again in Hadad's palm. He would have loved to pop it into his mouth. But someone else might see him and question him. He thrust his closed fist into his pocket, found the bottle of eye drops there, tucked away during the heat of the conversation, never paid for, almost forgotten. The plant was still tucked under his right arm, his right hand thrust into his jacket pocket to hide his wound. He found himself bound. He could not remove his right hand from his pocket without first removing the plant from the crook of his arm. To do that he would have to use his left hand. To use his left hand, he would have to eliminate the cockroach.

He was hungry.

He fished in his pocket, then popped the roach in his mouth, hoping that anyone watching him would figure he had just eaten a piece of candy. No one noticed. No one cared.

There was a difference as the group dispersed this second time. The first time what they had accomplished was saying they needed to do something. This second group *had* done something. There was a sense that some plan had been designed, that they were each satisfied.

The men gathered, regrouped, finished their business, and began to leave the store. The older lady went back across the street, around the fountain, and up the steps into the old courthouse. The girl sorted through her leathers, packed up the ones that she was taking along, stacked the rest neatly on the counter. She was the last one in the store as Hadad went to the counter, put the eye drops down, set down the plant, and reached for his wallet. She smiled at him as she picked up her satchel and backed away from the counter toward the door, still smiling.

She backed into the Visitor as he came in the door.

Hadad had not seen him coming.

There are moments when the world is full of wonder, when the smile of one person can turn the clarity of the scene around one into the mist of dawn over a mountain lake. And when in the next moment one's very existence is threatened, the harsh contrast makes the threat ever so much more potent.

All Hadad could manage was to not blink. His body froze, his pulse raced, his muscles gripped his organs and locked. He stared.

The Visitor brushed past the girl, unimpeded by her, and headed straight for Hadad. He was not in uniform. He was dressed exactly as Hadad was: a flannel shirt, jeans, a jacket. Disguised, he had walked down the street and into the store without alarming anyone. Anyone except Hadad. He grinned and started to laugh and then to speak.

"Gclixtchp! Truqch klzopltx grbpdtiq? Spriqktz plictx klzopltx plafqzkrsm. Zhrnimpt trlipgt qravcprts. Crizlchsqpts!"

Chapter 3

"How dare you spit at him!" The girl spoke and Hadad looked at her. She did not know. She did not recognize the Visitor for who he was. She had recognized only the hostility.

"Spit at him! You're crazy, lady. I wasn't spitting at him. I was talking to him. He's one of us." The Visitor started to laugh, the cynical, brittle laugh that had been part of his whole presence since he had entered the store.

"You're wrong, mister. You couldn't be further from the truth. I don't know who you think he is, but you're wrong."

Hadad recognized the truth beyond her words. She did not know who the Visitor thought he was. She was defending him merely because he had been attacked.

"Gclixtchp, plupltle," the Visitor challenged Hadad to reveal himself. But Hadad wasn't watching him. He was watching the girl, watching as she gradually became aware of the significance of the words, watching as she gradually realized she was addressing an alien, watching as she bypassed her own fear and gathered all the tension of the moment into a counterattack.

"You push in here as if you owned the place. Well, you are mistaken, mister. You think you're entitled to something, but you've got no right to anything but the air you breathe. And I'm not real certain you're entitled to that. You owe me an apology for pushing me and him an apology for spitting at him and I want to hear one now."

"I'm just talking the only language this man knows. He's one of us. He's got you fooled. He's one of us and not only that, when they find out he's here, somebody is going to be very, very pleased."

"You're wrong, mister." The Visitor wasn't convinced. "I've known this man all my life. In a couple weeks we are going to be married, and this kid I'm carrying is one-hundred-percent human. Whoever you think he is, you're wrong." The arrogance left the Visitor's face. It seemed like he had bought her story and now felt foolish and exposed for his error. "It's time for those apologies, mister. Let's hear them."

The Visitor looked first at Hadad, then at the girl, then back at Hadad, and then at the floor. He mumbled rather than spoke and all that came out was "So I made a mistake."

And then he was gone.

They watched as he left the store, looked up and down the street, and then turned to the left and disappeared into the gas-station lot next door. The atmosphere in the store was still charged with the encounter, and it was a long pause before anyone moved or said anything.

"Thank you."

Hadad was the first to speak. His words hung in the air and were punctuated by silence.

The girl turned and for the first time Hadad realized that she was looking him evenly in the eye. She was as tall as he was, and stood straight, unblushing, unblinking, as confident as any of the women commanders he had known on his own planet, on the ships. He had not seen women among the Earth ones who were like that.

"Thank you."

"I may have just saved your life. I understand when they spit like that, it's venomous. You could have died."

"I did not know that. Thank you."

Hadad did not know what to say. His muscles were no longer frozen in fear, but he still could not move. His pulse had calmed from the attack of the previous moment, but it was not less intense. He did not want to look away from the soft "eyes of a deer," and so he stared.

It was she who looked away, broke the intensity of the prolonged moment.

"Look, we just got engaged. Maybe we ought to get to know each other. How about lunch?"

Hadad started to object.

"My invite, my treat. I pick up the check. I insist."

Hadad looked at the floor, tried to pull away.

"We're in this fight together. I really would like to know who you are. Please."

Hadad looked up into her eyes. Then he smiled and nodded.

"Good. There's a nice place I know right down the street. Used to be a family restaurant until a friend of mine bought it. She always wanted to open a vegetarian restaurant. She's practically going broke in this meat-and-potatoes town. We may be her only customers. Come on."

"Be careful out on the street. We don't know how many Visitors we have now." The voice of the manager broke into their conversation and Hadad became aware that someone else was in the store. Gradually he became aware that he, too, was in the store, that there was a real world of Prineville, a real threat of invasion of his territory.

"We sure will. Thanks for the reminder, as if I needed it after dealing with that creep. They make my blood run cold. Just the thought of a lizard under that comfortably familiar exterior! I sure don't need any encouragement not to cooperate with *them*." The girl opened the door as she talked, and though she had started the conversation addressing the manager, by the end she was speaking to Hadad as they stepped out into the street.

There were no Visitors in sight. The traffic was normal and light. A few people were going into stores or offices. For the most part the town looked still. Third Street, because it was the highway through town, was always a little busier than the other avenues, but it wasn't crowded.

The restaurant was in the next block and across the street. When they had walked a hundred yards or so, the girl slipped her hand under Hadad's arm. They walked in step, her strides long enough that Hadad was not uncomfortable adjusting to her rhythm.

"I guess we really ought to start with names. I don't even know what to call you."

"The men at the mill call me Arab."

"That's not your name, is it?"

"No. They just called me that because I didn't know English."

"You're not American, then."

"No. But I have an American name."

"What is it?"

"David. Most people call me Dave."

"Dave. David . . . David what?"

"You are only the second person to ask me that. Mr. Ripley asked that when I went to work for him."

"I don't understand."

"David is my American name. My name before was Hadad. That is the name I was given, when I was to be—" He stopped, realizing he was saying too much, realizing that he had never before in his life wanted to tell anyone about himself.

"When you were to be what?" The girl pushed for an answer. She seemed to really want to know. Hadad tried to think of a way to tell her the truth without saying too much.

They reached the corner and crossed the street. She still held his arm. When they reached the other curb it was easier to talk again.

"I was named after an ancient king, because they wanted me to be a great leader here on Earth."

"Wow. That's a heavy load for a kid to carry. What brought you to America instead?"

"A political decision."

"And there goes the kingdom down the drain, eh?"

Hadad laughed. She was easy to talk to.

"And what about you? What is your name?"

"Ruth. You know, 'Whither thou goest I will go' and all that jazz." She pulled away from him toward the curb. He followed. They stepped between the parked cars into the traffic and when it was clear, crossed to the restaurant on the other side.

"I don't know 'Whither thou goest I will go and all that jazz.' What does that mean?"

"Ruth—from the Bible. She left her family and country to go to Judah with her mother-in-law after her husband died. Loyalty. That sort of stuff."

"I see. And are you loyal, that sort of stuff?"

"I don't know. I guess so. In my own way, I guess I am."

The restaurant was small. Plywood partitioned the tables in the front from a kitchen in the back. A picture of women picking in a field was thumbtacked in the center of the wood. Three long narrow tables stretched into the room from the windows at the front with three chairs on each side—hard wooden chairs, with curved loops of wood for backrests. The tables were covered with white-linen cloths, rough-woven, and darned where they had been torn, but clean and very white.

They were the only customers.

"Hi, Ruth." The lady who bounced out from the kitchen with menus in her hand identified herself quickly as Ruth's friend, the owner of the establishment. She stood about five foot five and though her hair was cut short in front, it fell behind her to her waist. She came over to Ruth and wrapped her arms around her in a familiar hug, disappearing into the chest and arms that enfolded her, and then awkwardly extracting her hair as she pulled away and the strands caught in the buttons and rough texture of Ruth's jacket.

"Betty, I'd like you to meet my friend, Hadad."

"Who?"

"That is my family name. It is hard for Americans. You can call me David."

"Okay, David. What did she say your name was?"

"Hadad." He said the name slowly.

"Okay. I'll call you David. So what would you all like to eat today? I've got lots of food."

"Seriously, how's it going?"

"Well, if I get a couple more customers today, I should be able to open tomorrow."

"That bad, really?"

"Sit down, Ruth. You don't have to worry about my business troubles. You're doing all you can. You're my best customer. I knew it was a gamble when I opened. And I'm doing what I want to do. If this doesn't work, I'll do something else. But at least I will have tried something that was important to me. What can I say? Now, what do you want to eat?"

"I'll start with some carrot juice while I read the menu. How about you, Hadad? She juices it fresh. It's the best."

"Just water, thank you."

"One carrot juice, one water, and two menus."

Betty gave them cards which were handwritten to serve as menus, then disappeared into the kitchen behind the plywood wall and the sounds of refrigerator doors and juicer gave them some privacy in which to decide what they would eat.

Hadad put his plant in the middle of the table.

"I meant to ask you about that. What is it? Why are you carrying it around with you?"

"It is a medicine plant. I don't know its American name."

"I'll look it up in my Culpeppers. If it's medicinal, it should be listed in there. What do you use it for?"

Hadad was not certain that the use he had in mind would relate to humans. He was cautious. Again, he did not want to lie. But he was hesitant with the truth.

"It makes the surface go back together."

"Surface? You mean skin."

"Yes. Skin."

"It has to be like an aloe vera then."

"I don't know. It is sticky."

They laughed.

"So, why are you carrying a medicine plant with you everywhere you go today?"

"I just paid for it at the store."

"Bob's?"

"No. At the Posie Shop."

"Oh. You just bought it."

"Yes. I just bought it."

"Do you . . . are you sick?"

"Just my hand." He took his right hand out of his pocket and showed her the bandage. It had slipped a little and there was a small line of green showing through the bandage. It bothered Hadad, and he quickly put his hand back into his pocket.

"No, that's okay. You don't have to hide it. The sight of blood doesn't bother me. What happened?"

"It was a root. I didn't see it. It cut me."

"Is it going to be all right? I mean, is there anything I can do to help?"

"No. The medicine plant is all I need."

"How do you use it?"

Hadad did not want to say anything more. He had already said more than he felt comfortable sharing. He did not know how to change the subject. He did not know how to answer with a lie. He looked for a simple way to tell the truth.

"I grind it. I need tools. I have them at home."

"I'd like to watch you do that sometime."

Again the eyes focused on his. Again there was nothing to say. Again the silence made his breath still. Again he could only stare. Again it was she who looked away first.

Hadad was hungry.

And there was nothing on the menu he could possibly eat.

"My favorite is her lentil soup, and the sprouted bean salad is delicious. She grows her own sprouts. And can she fry tofu. I have to stay away from it though. I'm totally off fried foods. She's the only one who can get me to eat anything cooked. I hate to cook. Growing food, that's more my thing. I love to plant things and watch them grow. I'd live in a garden if I could get away with doing nothing else."

"You do. All of Earth is a garden."

"Yeah. I suppose that is one way of looking at it."

"Now, what are you lovely people going to have for lunch today?"

"I'm in a rut, Betty. I'm going to have another sprouted salad."

"Okay. How about you, David?"

"Whatever she has."

"Two sprouted salads it is."

Hadad looked around the restaurant. There had been a cockroach in the store. Perhaps he could find another here and figure out some way to catch it and eat it without appearing too strange to his hostess. The corners were clean. Everything was clean. He saw a door marked Gentlemen at the rear next to the screen door that led out the back. He excused himself from the table and went back to the men's room.

There were no water bugs around the plumbing. He had hoped, but found nothing. Perhaps in back. He turned to the screen door as he came out of the men's room. There were flies buzzing the door. He opened it, went out, and grabbed a half dozen from the air, stuffing them into his mouth as he caught them and reaching for more.

Betty came out from the kitchen and saw him through the screen.

"Oh, you don't have to worry about those flies, David. I have an electronic zapper. Keeps all the insects out of here. I couldn't get along without it."

A few flies weren't going to solve the hunger problem, but to go any further would be rude. He would have to wait. Hadad returned to the table and looked over the tossed salad. It looked like grass pulled up, seed and all.

Ruth poured the creamy dressing over her salad and began to eat, talking between mouthfuls, caught up in the excitement of the conversation.

For a while it was possible for Hadad to forget the tension of the day, to forget the presence of the ship, the threat his former blood brother and friend had made back at the store. It was possible to see only the excitement of this girl and all she talked about. He picked at the grasses selectively and listened to her stories. For a while.

". . . totally on raw foods. It works. I lived there for a while and learned all about it. I have all the credentials. I work with it a lot. I've done a lot of therapies: acupressure, rolfing, touch healing, chiropractic. They all help, that's for sure. Most of the people just think I'm a kook. They laugh at what I do.

But some people listen. And they get better. You might have difficulty accepting this, but I could heal your hand with touch if you would let me."

The eyes looked at him. This time Hadad looked away.

Hadad glanced out the window, automatically seeking the outside rather than run the risk of self-revelation inside. The town was shifting in its normal rhythms, a little slowed by the presence of the mother ship, but the only noticeable difference was that people on the street watched the ship as they walked, watched it as they crossed from office to office, watched it as they took a break from the routine and came outside for a breath of air. Humans seldom look up. Today they all did.

The Visitor in the store had been Jeffrey. At one time they had been classmates. They had come from the same community at home, recruited the same day. They had heard the promises of fame and glory and conquest at the same lecture. They spoke the same dialect. They had chosen the same planetary project. They had been friends. Until Hadad had been chosen to lead the expedition and Jeffrey had been overlooked for another project, and placed as his assistant. Spligxzt was Jeffrey's true name. It meant "The Jealous One."

It had been hard to lead a friend. It had been hard to be a friend to one who could not follow. When the plans diverted them from the original mission, Jeffrey had gloated. And perhaps friendship could have been restored if they had been given separate duties on the new project. They still had so much they had shared. But when Hadad was put in charge of the program to maintain the storage system of human packages, Jeffrey had been made his assistant. And that was more than their bonds of friendship could sustain.

They had done their work. Jeffrey had followed orders. But they had never again spoken as buddies.

The message Jeffrey had jeered at him was the final coup in the intense battle for supremacy that Jeffrey had waged with him, that Hadad had surrendered to. Jeffrey wanted power and glory. He did not have power or glory. Hadad did not want either, and aboard the ship, before Diana had changed their targeted destination on Earth, he had had them both. When Hadad had left for the compound in Los Angeles, relieved of his post on the mother ship, Jeffrey had been given his shipboard position; that had, at last, given Jeffrey power. Now he could have his glory. The message he delivered was that Diana had given orders that Hadad was to be shot on sight as a traitor. Jeffrey had found him. He would be rewarded for the information that "the despicable one" was on Earth.

It had seemed that Jeffrey had accepted Ruth's story. But Hadad wasn't sure. He did not know how many others from this ship would recognize him. It was not Diana's ship. That was clear from Jeffrey's message. But how many of the troops would he know, would know him? And how sympathetic were the commanders with Diana's personal vendetta against him? He had defied *her*, not the whole service. But would anyone know that?

"What do you do down at the mill?"

The question brought him back from his reverie, back to the table, back to the eyes of the deer.

Hadad shook his head.

"I said, what do you do down at the mill?"

"I sweep. Sometimes I carry things. Heavy things."

"I thought you said you were going to be a king. That doesn't sound like the sort of things kings are trained to do. What did you do before you came here?"

"I . . ." Hadad laughed, seeing the craziness in what he would be describing if he told the truth. "I . . ." He laughed again.

"This had better be a good one. What did you do? Guard hordes of beautiful maidens in the holds of slave ships? Do battle with Amazon queens for power and control of empires? Program giant computers so that with the flip of a switch only you could touch you could destroy or preserve the lives of millions? What did you do, for heaven's sake, that's so funny?"

"All of those things and a few more."

Ruth laughed, and the laugh was contagious. They fed on each other's enjoyment and on the outrageousness of the idea, she that he could say he did those things, he that she could describe so accurately his truth without knowing she had done so.

When the laughter had let loose of them, and they had caught their breath, she asked again: "Seriously, now. I cannot imagine a man who was trained to lead a nation being content all his life pushing a broom. What are you trained to do? What kind of position *did* you have before you came here?"

"I can't answer that question simply. To learn to lead, you must learn how to be in front of people. To lead them you must find out what direction they are going and get there first. To lead a nation is not to be different from the nation. It is only to know what the nation is and to let it be that. It is no different pushing a broom. Except that to push a broom, you must learn to follow. But I haven't answered your question. One of the things I did was to program computers, as you said."

"Then why didn't you get a job here programming computers? There's a whole room of computers at the courthouse, and I know they need good programmers."

"What do you know about computers?"

"Not much. I've done data entry. I worked at a university doing that. I've never programmed one, if that's what you mean."

"Okay. Most work with computers for most people is 'data entry,' as you call it. The rest of it is figuring out how to make the circuitry of a machine that is very simple do what someone wants done. When I came to Prineville, I could have learned to work with the computers. They are all different. But they are all alike. Ours are basically not so different from yours. I had no problem in Los Angeles when I had to use the computers at the compound. The problem was not the computers. The problem was I did not speak American. I still do not do good at speaking. But then I did not know the words. In order for me to work I would need to know what someone wanted the computer to do that it could not already do. They would have to explain it in American. If they could explain it in 'computer' they would not need me."

"And so you pushed a broom."

"And so I pushed a broom. Because they could explain that without the words I did not know."

"Doesn't it frustrate you to not be using your mind?"

"What does it mean, 'frustrate'?"

"That's a hard one. I don't know. Make you upset, angry."

"And what does it mean 'not to be using your mind'?"

"Not creating, not solving problems, not doing something important—I don't know."

"I do not think I have ever not used my mind. Perhaps when I have the experience I can let you know if it makes me upset or angry."

Ruth laughed again, but this time Hadad did not see the joke, not even his own version of the joke.

"You sound like a Zen master."

"What is a Zen master?"

"Zen masters are teachers who teach by asking questions like what is the sound of one hand clapping?"

"But that is the sound of silence. I do not understand what is so difficult about that, or funny."

"And you are the only person I have ever known who has responded to that question without a second thought. You are either very foolish or very wise."

"If the word is the one I think it is, I think I am very foolish. You said you had done data entry for something called a university. What is that?"

"It's a school. In America it is the most advanced school."

"Then you were a student."

"Yes. Among other things."

"What other things?"

"Oh, I've done lots of things: I studied art history at the university. I loved the history part. But I had a lot of trouble with the criticism. I just didn't have the same value system as the professor did. Got me in a lot of trouble. So I was an actress for a while, in Los Angeles. I made a film once. That was okay. I was a folksinger in San Francisco for a long time, but I got tired of always being in front of people. New people every night, a few regulars. Pretty soon I got the feeling nobody even heard what I was singing. I wasn't touching people anymore. So I traveled, worked with healers. Once I taught in a special school for children who were deaf. That's probably the most important thing I've ever done. Since then I've lived by the things I make. Now I make leather goods. Before, I painted. Before that, I threw pots."

"Who did you throw pots at?"

"No, no. I didn't throw pots at people. That's what they call it when you make pots out of clay."

"Oh, I see."

"I'll show you sometime."

Again the eyes caught him. Again he did not know what he was supposed to say, what he could say, what he wanted to say. There was a moment when there was nothing in the world except the look in her eyes. He stared. After a while she looked away.

"Mostly I . . . I guess I'm sort of a mixture," she began again. "When I'm working with people, I get tired of having people around all the time. And when I work alone, I get lonely. That's why I quit the computer job. I never really talked to anyone." She looked up at him; this time she did not look that special way.

Hadad looked out the window again at the people. He was restless with the waiting, waiting for something to happen that would make the threat more tangible or make it go away.

"You haven't eaten much."

"What? . . . Oh, no, I'm sorry."

"That's all right. Different people worry in different ways. I eat."

"What?"

"When I'm worried or frightened, I eat. Some people can't eat when they are frightened."

"Oh."

"We haven't talked about it."

"Eating?"

"No, the Visitors."

"No."

"Are we all going to be taken up in that ship and served for their dinners?"

"I don't know."

"Why are they here? They weren't here before. I thought from the reports on the freedom network that we were safe up here. Lots of people have come to

Oregon because it was safer. Why are they here all of a sudden?"

"I have asked the same question. I have also asked why they have not come before."

"Because of the red dust."

"Exactly. But now they are here."

"How can they exist here?"

Hadad looked at her. He wondered how much he should tell her of his thoughts, of his assessments. How much could he tell her without revealing who he was? He had an answer to her question. He chose his words carefully.

"There are two explanations possible. First, the red dust might not be effective here; it might be dormant."

"That's not possible. It's too cold here. I heard the report on the freedom network. The virus stays alive if it can hibernate, if it's cold enough."

"Second, it is possible that they have been working on a vaccine, an antidote. If they have found one, then they would have to find a place to test it."

"A place with red dust."

"A place where they thought there was red dust."

"Then they might not be after us."

"You cannot trust that thought. Everyone must protect himself from being taken on the ship, from being taken in the trucks, from being taken to the processing."

"Do you know what they do?"

"Yes."

"I've heard it's awful."

"Ruth, why do you not eat meat?"

"Because I—" She hesitated. "I was going to say because I reverence life. But before I learned what my body needs, I used to eat meat. And I had just as much reverence for life then. I have reverence for the life of the carrot I just ate. I guess . . ."

"Is it awful for the carrot to be made into your juice?"

"I suppose it would be if the carrot were not willing to be made into my juice."

"And how do you know the carrot is willing?"

"I guess I just believe it is supposed to be willing. I don't know."

"For the Visitors"—Hadad said the word cautiously—"it is right for them to prepare their food. For the food comes the choice whether it is to be willing or not. If it is willing, it is not an awful process. If it is unwilling, then the food tastes of the fear."

"How do you know that?"

"Because I know about food. That is one of the things I am trained about to be a king."

"Is Mr. Ripley right that we have to kill the Visitors to protect ourselves?"

"He is right. And the other man is right. It is not necessary just to kill. To kill is to live always in fear. It is also necessary to make them go away."

"How do we do that?"

"There is something no one knows. Something you must not tell to the wrong people. Something that would make everyone here even more frightened, and worse, could put the people here in even more danger."

"Who are the right people?"

"I do not know. That is why I must tell *you*. I . . . my American is too clumsy, I would make a mistake."

"What are you talking about?"

"Ruth, I know something about Prineville that makes it very dangerous for the Visitors to be here. Dangerous for you, not for them."

"What do you know about Prineville?"

"There is no red dust in this valley. I do not know how far the space extends that is uncontainerated."

"You mean uncontaminated."

"Yes."

"How do you know?"

"That is one of the other things I do . . ."

". . . to be a king."

"No, to be alive."

"You mean a job? Who are you working for? Why are they studying Prineville? Who sent you here?"

"No. You follow the wrong rail."

"You mean wrong track." Ruth started to laugh in spite of herself and in spite of the seriousness of her interest in what she was now learning.

"When the red dust was first spread into the winds to carry it all over the country, none of the dust was released into the winds that reached this part of the high desert. I waited for it to come. It did not come. The other way it has not come yet either."

"What do you mean?"

"The red dust is a virus. It will grow in the cells of the animals that have breathed it. It will not hurt humans. It will not hurt animals. But it will continue to grow. If the Visitors eat the meat of the animals who have breathed the live virus, then they will die, even if the red dust is no longer in the air."

"It works two ways then."

"Yes. It is worst for the Visitors to breathe the dust themselves. That is to be dead right away. It is slower the other way."

"They have stopped dusting in a lot of places. They used to announce it on the freedom network. They don't announce the dustings anymore."

"Since the dust does not harm Earth ones, it is no reason to stop. The only reason to stop must be because the Visitors cannot use the meat of the ones who have the virus, and so those Earth ones are safe.

That is the only logic that makes reason to stop the dustings."

"But you said—"

"That is right. The virus has not reached the cells of the animals here. That is the information you must tell no one. If the Visitors were to find that out, then they would collect the people here as food. If they think you have the virus, they may not want to contaminate the food-storage systems. You may be safe."

"How do you know the virus has not reached the animals, for that matter, the people?"

"About all the people I do not know. About the animals I know only the ones I have . . . tested."

"And that's why you're here?"

"Yes, that is why I am here."

"Who sent you?"

"No one sent me. I . . .." Here it became hard for Hadad to fit his truth with the limits of the words he had to use.

"Are you part of the resistance?"

"No."

"Who do you work for?"

"Ruth, this is not important. I want to know. I wanted to know because I cannot go home. Prineville is like my home, at least a little. I wanted to know because I wanted to know if it is safe for Prineville. I do not want to have to run away like the man, Joe, was saying."

"How did you get to be a king without being trained to fight?"

Hadad smiled. "I never got to be a king."

"That's right. I forgot. Somehow I sort of ran it all together. About you being a king. I never knew anyone who was going to be a king before."

"You don't know anyone who is going to be a king now."

"That's true."

"Will you run away from the Visitors?"

"Prineville is home. I do not know where to go."

"You told me about the red dust for a reason. Who am I supposed to tell?"

"As long as the Visitors send just one or two from the ship to look around, they will never find out about the food supply and you are safe. If I am right, they will test their antidote, and find that it works. That will mean they can invade the parts of the country that are cold, where the virus remains. Then they will start to work on the food processing. But that gives you some time."

"But their antidote might not be working. It's not a true test."

"That's right. But they don't know that yet. They must never find out. You must find the resistance in Los Angeles. You must convince them to dust the high desert."

"And the antidote?"

"If it works, then there is nothing that can save Prineville anyway. All you will have bought is time. But it may be time you need to find another solution. If the antidote fails, then they will leave."

"How will we have bought time?"

"To make enough antidote for the entire ship to stay in the area for a long period will take time. For a test, it is simple. But for living with the virus, they will need to build a plant to produce the antidote in quantity."

"But wouldn't they do that anyway, even without the red dust? Wouldn't they just assume that the antidote is working and start producing it?"

"You call that 'bluff,' right?"

"Yes, we call that 'bluff.'"

"Bluff works only when someone is afraid of consequences. The Visitors are not afraid of consequences."

"What do you mean?"

"If a man goes into a bank and says, 'I have a gun in my pocket. Give me the money or I will shoot,' the person has to decide if it is real, the threat, or just bluff. If he thinks it is real, he gives him the money. If he thinks it is bluff, he stalls and sets off the alarm to call the police. That is what they say on the television programs."

"Yeah, it sort of works that way."

"But if the person with the money is frightened he will die, then he will give the money, right?"

"That's the idea."

"No one likes to die. But . . ." Hadad became very quiet. He had never spoken before to an Earth one about the power of Zon. He had never spoken to one of his own people about Zon. One does not speak of the power one knows all one's life. One has no need to name that which surrounds one, contains one, sustains all being of all that one knows. He did not know the words that would say all that he wanted Ruth to understand. "It is different when you are not afraid to die. Humans are afraid to die."

"You said 'humans,' not 'Earth ones.'"

"Not all Earth ones are afraid to die. Some are. Most humans are."

"But the Visitors aren't?"

"No, Ruth. There is no fear."

"How do you know all this?"

"I was in Los Angeles. I worked for . . . I worked for Diana."

"But you said you weren't part of the resistance."

"There were a lot of us in Los Angeles who worked for Diana. Some were part of the resistance. The rest of us were just doing the jobs we had always done."

"I didn't know they used civilians."

"There were lots of civilians at the compound."

"But how could you be part of it and not . . ."

Hadad looked at Ruth. The eyes of the deer were frightened and shaming. He looked at her with no defense, as he had looked at the coyote for the entire night, never giving up the right he had claimed to be exactly what he was, exactly where he was, exactly who he was. She looked down at the table and then back up to his face, then to his eyes.

"Ruth, I am not a brave man."

She looked back to the table. In a moment she breathed a heavy sigh.

"Then you think they will test—"

"If a Visitor can walk through town safely with the antidote, the next test will be to see if another can walk through town safely without the antidote. If he dies, then they will know the antidote works. Nothing short of that will satisfy them. If they find out soon there is no red dust in the atmosphere, they will invade Prineville."

"They haven't invaded yet."

"Yet."

For a moment she did not say anything. Then she sighed and her shoulders dropped.

"I'm going to the Ladies. I'll be right back."

Ruth pushed her chair back from the table and got up. The energy Hadad had noticed earlier in her movements was gone. There was instead a lethargy, a despondency, that seemed foreign to her. Betty passed her, coming from the kitchen as Ruth went to the other door in the narrow hallway.

"You two sure had some heavy talking to do. You old friends?"

"No, we just meet."

"You're not new in town."

"Not this morning new."

"Ah, I didn't mean that." Betty started to laugh as she got the inference that he was making. "I mean, you're not a visitor in town or nothin' like that."

"You think I am a Visitor?"

"You're teasing me. You know I didn't mean that."

"Why do you ask?"

"Thought I'd seen you round the mill."

"You might have seen me. I work there."

"Then I *have* seen you before. My husband works there."

"And who is your husband?"

"John Hanawald."

"I know him."

"That's where I've seen you, then."

Ruth came back to the table.

"I'll pay that, Betty. David's my guest this time."

Hadad looked up and the eyes of the deer returned his look with that strange stare that made him stare back, unaware of time and circumstance. Ruth looked away and gave Betty money for their lunch.

They left the restaurant and walked back on that side of the street, back toward the courthouse, walking east, looking at the ship hanging in the sky. They didn't talk much. This time Ruth didn't take his arm.

"What is the meaning, 'heritage'?"

"Why do you ask?"

"Come here. I will show you." Hadad took Ruth by the arm and led her the half block more to the fountain in front of the courthouse. "Here." He pointed to the sign on the base of the fountain: "The heritage of the past is the seed that brings forth the harvest of the future."

"It's like a gift, I guess. More than that, though. It's like everything that has ever been, that has ever been valued, that people have put energy and love into that they can pass on to their kids and their grandkids."

"Things then."

"Things, and traditions."

"It is very special to value things that are old, ideas that are old. Not everyone is like that."

Ruth looked up in the sky.

"They do not value old things, or old ideas."

"I had a feeling that was what you were talking about."

"Thank you for the lunch. I am sorry I could not eat."

"I understand. The food wasn't what was important anyway. Where . . . where are you headed now?"

"I don't know."

"We forgot your plant." Ruth's energy returned rapidly.

"Oh, yes." Hadad felt the urgency from her and assumed it himself. "I must go back to get it. Then I . . ."

"Well, my car's over there."

"I have to get my plant."

"Yeah."

"You will be careful with what I told you?"

"Sure. I . . . I don't know . . . I'll see you sometime."

"You will travel safely?"

"Oh, sure."

"About what you said to the Visitor . . ."

"What about it?"

"Thank you."

"Oh, that. Sure. You owe me one. One of these days you get to rescue me."

"I promise."

The eyes of the deer looked once more at him and the urgencies of the plant, the day, were gone again. Something drew him toward her, but his muscles stopped him from moving. Suddenly Ruth smiled and the look was gone. And then as suddenly she stepped from the curb and began to run toward her car.

The tires squealed, the horn blared, and the bumper impacted Ruth's leg with a thump. She was pushed down the street by the car as it stopped, and then it dropped her on the pavement.

Chapter 4

Paul stood at the console behind Eleanor when the guards dragged the costumed Jeffrey into her quarters. He was amazed at the beleaguered look on the lieutenant commander's face when he became aware that they had been alone. Eleanor was, to Jeffrey's mind, to be his own prize. He did not cherish the notion that Paul might have taken advantage of his absence.

Eleanor was a toy to Paul. It was true, he enjoyed playing from time to time. But for him she was no prize, no conquest, and he kept his values very clear when it came to the politics of the bedroom. He had won his military command of *this* ship by bedding Diana well. When she had gained strategic power she had remembered him and counted on his allegiance. Now that he had gained her favors, he would have her and no others. At least no others as public and conspicuous as Eleanor.

But it did not pass his notice that his friendship with Eleanor was interpreted as a threat to Jeffrey. That pleased him. He did not like the lieutenant commander and enjoyed any irritation that he might be able to inflict upon him.

Eleanor was a scientist, not a strategist. She had evolved a strain of volatile antitoxin that seemed to hold the resistance virus, the V-dust, at bay for a couple of hours. She was refining it to develop a true antitoxin, when her experiments were sabotaged by fifth columnists. Only Paul had known enough to sabotage the experiments. Only he had known exactly what stage she had reached in her work, the precise moment when a bit too much acid would void the entire project. But Eleanor was not a strategist and had never reasoned out the source of her aggravation. She would have to begin again. But in the meanwhile the volatile antitoxin allowed them to penetrate infested areas for three hours at a time without harmful effect. Each returning combatant had to be sanitized to return to the ship, and each could not be reinjected for seventy-two hours. And eventually the body would saturate with antitoxin and become ill from the solution itself. But it was the best they could do for now.

Jeffrey stood staring wistfully at Eleanor.

"Leave him," she barked at the guards.

They turned and left her compartment. Paul poured himself a glass of mulled caterpillar.

"All right, Jeffrey," Eleanor began, "what have you discovered in your masquerade? I'm still not satisfied that this hoax was really necessary. And it certainly is undignified. You look like a common Earthling. Why I even agreed to consent to this, I'm not certain."

Jeffrey regained his swagger once his bodyguards had been dismissed. Paul was delighted that he had disconcerted his contender by ordering the escort. He knew now that Jeffrey was unable to bear an escort with authority. And that pleased him. The Jealous One—Jeffrey certainly lived up to his true name. He had tried to reach Diana with his intrigue, to sabotage Paul's prospects while they were both on Lydia's Los Angeles ship.

But Jeffrey was an upstart, vengeful. He lacked savoir-faire. And especially he lacked tact. Already he had offended Eleanor by overriding her plan to send an inoculated troop into the hills to test the antitoxin. Instead, he had insisted only one should go—and of course he was to be the volunteer. Heroics are either dangerous or stupid. Jeffrey's heroics were generally stupid.

Paul listened as Eleanor now berated him for his departure from the craft area, leaving his hover craft untended. It seems he had gone down to the planet, left his craft, obscured but untended, stolen clothes and gone into town to see just how far he could penetrate the populace without notice. Apparently he had been successful. But the risk of capture, of inciting resistance, of being killed in the process, could have defeated the test of the antitoxin. Eleanor was not interested in his reconnaissance ventures. She wanted to know how he fared with the virus. She wanted a specimen from his colon to test in her laboratory and she was impatient that he had kept her waiting.

Paul watched. Had he left, Jeffrey could have sweet-talked his way around the angered Eleanor. But Paul did not leave. And so Jeffrey took the verbal abuse and argued his cause with logic rather than sex and came up wanting of arguments. At least for Eleanor.

"You might be interested, Paul, in one bit of information I gathered." Jeffrey turned away from Eleanor now and addressed him directly. "We aren't the only Visitors in Central Oregon."

Paul lifted an eyebrow almost involuntarily.

"I'm sure you will remember Hadad—The Leader's chosen disciple at the compound at home, the future king of Pau. I always figured he was killed with Stephen in Los Angeles. But I was wrong. Somehow he got to Oregon. I have a feeling Diana will be very pleased to know where he is. And very pleased with whomever it is who carries out her orders to eliminate him. Apparently he was part of the fifth column, otherwise how could he have survived the V-dust? I'd say that makes him doubly fair game."

Paul shrugged, unwilling to reveal his response to

the information. Hadad had been a pawn, first of The Leader, then of Diana. But it had seemed to Paul that Hadad was liked by The Leader. If he were still alive, he might serve Paul's interest. He would have to consider carefully.

Since he had aligned himself with the fifth column, Paul had complicated his strategic efforts. Now he must weigh his priorities.

"And you, Jeffrey, you, too, were in Los Angeles. Were you a part of the fifth column? Is that how you survived the V-dust?"

Jeffrey bristled at the accusation. Paul was amused that words, even false words, could reach their mark.

"You know I was on the mother ship and taken prisoner. You were the one who negotiated for our release."

"Of course. I had . . . forgotten."

Paul had had enough; Jeffrey had suffered his presence sufficiently for one day. He downed the last of his drink, nodded to them both, and left Eleanor's quarters.

The long white corridors of the mother ship gave Paul no solace though they were his to control, to dominate. His orders could change the path of any armed party, the priority of any worker, the execution of any plan designed by a junior officer. His authority was complete and tested.

But that authority rested upon his compliance with the western invasion. Diana's plan was simple: vanquish Earth. The Leader had designed a much more complex invasion. His priority had been relief for the famine and drought at home. His plan had included overcoming petty Earth allegiances, molding the populace to serve his purposes, taking what was needed and leaving the rest under the supervision of devoted followers—intelligent, docile priests—who would govern the remaining Earthlings and mold them into passive, obedient creatures, available for the future needs of their superiors, disinterested in retaliation or rebellion. The priests of Zon had been eliminated. Only Amon remained, and his influence had been repressed, his followers forced into obedience to The Leader.

But the quality of priesthood remained among the people. And The Leader had found that a useful commodity. No longer priests of Zon, the young trainees would become the priests of The Leader. And so he had sought out fifty young men, all of whom bore the mark of Zon, and had trained them in the new ways of the new priesthood. He had banned the book of Zon, replaced it with the book of The Leader. He had taken the sacred language and indoctrinated his new priests with new meanings for the sacred words. He had taught these young men how to lead people, promised they would become kings, and, using the conversion techniques, stripped from them the core of their belief system, the sense of worthiness that aligned them with the Lords of Light. He had created them as docile, accepting, empty shells and given them responsibility with no authority.

Diana had rebelled herself at the notion of leaving priests in charge of a population. She wanted the control herself and so, even before reaching Earth, she had undermined the allegiance of John and the other directors, changed the objectives of each of the mother ships, and given herself the greatest advantage by choosing for her ship a megalopolis to conquer.

Paul hadn't needed the privacy of her bed to comprehend her tactics. But having enjoyed those pleasures, he had used that intimacy to learn her vulnerabilities. His loyalties were still with The Leader. He could not overcome Diana's influence directly. And so he had used her interest in him to gain position, and then he had sought out the fifth column and found among its ranks those sympathetic with his resistance to Diana's leadership.

He was valuable to them in his own position, but he found it difficult to keep close communication with the organizers on the ship. And he could not assume control of the fifth column. He would have liked that. But the allegiance of the rebellion aboard his ship was already with Justine. And so he contented himself with facilitating the plans she directed, aware that in time he must, for his own purposes, subvert her to his plan, or eliminate her influence.

Power over one ship was not enough to satisfy Paul. He wanted Diana's power, and ultimately he wanted the power of The Leader.

He passed Patricia in the corridor and gave the obscure signal that would call her to his quarters for a private conversation. She nodded in acknowledgment and continued down the corridor without breaking stride. Now he must return to his quarters and wait until she found time and excuse to visit him. She was careful and that is why he had chosen her for his personal liaison. He could not risk detection of his counterallegiance. He must appear loyal to Diana and her cause.

He wondered now what course best served his purpose.

The Leader's priests had been eliminated. It was assumed that Hadad had been killed in Los Angeles and so he had not been considered in the purge. It was evident now that he had known in advance what would happen and had escaped.

The first thing Paul must determine was if Hadad had aligned with the resistance. If not, he must be absorbed into the fifth-column operations, or he must be eliminated. It would not serve Paul's purposes to have a third Visitor interest in Earth. But would Hadad serve the resistance? He wasn't sure.

He reached his quarters and set the visual monitors onto prerecorded scenes of himself undressing, sleeping, reading, enjoying the privacy of his own compartment. He turned down the lighting in the room and removed his uniform, preferring a vestment of fur for the communication with Patricia that would come soon.

He pushed aside the drape at the far end of the room, exposing his bed. He threw additional pillows onto the sheepskin cover and stretched out to enjoy the wait. He reached over his head to the pile of books he kept beside him. He had cultured the habit of reading while at the compound in Los Angeles. The books of Earth were such fascinating relics of a dead past. The mysteries of the culture fascinated him. He took the top book: *The Art of War*, by Sun Tzu. That one would do nicely.

He opened the book to the place he'd marked, turned on the light behind him, and began to read.

Chapter 5

All of the human energies in witness of the impact of the car upon Ruth denied awareness of the moment; consumed themselves in wondering what they might have done in the moment before to avoid the accident; to warn her; to change the momentum of the car; to prevent the damage done that now could not, time being irreversible, be undone. Only Hadad did not try to rewrite history. And so he was the first person at Ruth's side when the car finally stopped and dropped her to the pavement.

Now it did not matter that his right hand was bandaged, hidden, torn. With both hands he straightened her body, feeling as he touched her the places where her body held the pain, her shoulders tensed, her elbows raw and bleeding, her back bruised, her head aching, her hips jarred, her leg broken, her feet burning. There were too many points of pain for him to attend to himself. But now there were people gathering. The driver was bringing a jacket from the car, tucking it under Ruth's head.

It was not that Hadad expected the people to know what he knew to do to help her. It was that he expected the people to know and do what *they* knew to do to help her. And what surprised him was that they did nothing. The driver cradled her head on the jacket and then knelt beside her saying over and over: "I didn't see you. Really, I didn't expect you to dash out like that. Are you going to be all right?" The others stood around in a circle pressing closer and closer. They spoke to one another; one man ran back to the store shouting: "Someone call an ambulance; she's hurt." But no one *did* anything.

And so the authority that Hadad had always expressed among his own people surfaced with these Earth ones. Easily he commanded. Easily he assigned tasks. Easily he evoked from others their cooperation and competence. And no one questioned his leadership because he did not question it himself.

To this one he gave directions on how to hold the places on Ruth's head that would allow her to feel and release her pain. To another he said: "Squeeze here, hard." And the person did. To another he said: "Put your finger here and press." To another he said: "Don't stop her from crying." To Ruth he said: "Remember now the energy released when the bone snapped in your leg. That is the energy you must receive back into your body." And as he guided her, he pressed on the regeneration points he found in her thigh and visualized the regeneration in her body, as he had always visualized it in his own, calling on all the assurance he had known since birth, known as natural to all living beings, known and seen on Earth in all the lizards he had caught for food, known as the way of Zon, learned as the teachings of Zon, practiced as a follower of Zon.

He took the "now," the realization of Ruth, broken. And in his mind he moved back through time, second by second, encompassing them all, back through the impact of her body on the pavement, back through the press of her body through the air, back through the twist and snap of her body as it responded to the impact, back to the impact, back to the squeal of brakes, back to the energy of running, back to the imbalance as she stepped from the curb, back to the engaging energy of her body standing before him on the curb.

And each of those thoughts he held, singularly, not

rushing, not hurrying to the next. Each he held until he felt her body under his hands accept the truth of his visualization. When her body accepted the impact on the pavement, Ruth cried, and the sobs wrenched from her body. A woman came over and tried to quiet her, but the man who had been told to let her cry chased the woman away. And then as her body remembered the momentary flight, Ruth stopped breathing. For long moments she neither exhaled or inhaled. Then the crowd grew frightened. A man exclaimed: "She's going to die." And another came over, shouting: "Tip her head back, let me in there." But just as he got to her she suddenly gasped, filling her lungs, then breathed deeply. And the man turned away confused, and frustrated that he was not needed for the only help he knew how to give.

As her body twisted in Hadad's mind, she moaned in agony. Again the muscles tightened and the body wrenched physically in response to the mental image. Now it was resisting. But he held the thought evenly, patiently, and finally the body accepted the truth of its experience.

An energy returned to it, and in a snap as abrupt as the impact of the car upon her leg, the broken bone rejoined and the cartilage knitted to reconstitute her leg. And then her body relaxed.

Hadad opened his eyes, looked down at Ruth, and then released the regeneration points. The work was done. He assured the others who were helping that she would be all right, and let them release their responsibilities. Ruth smiled, convincing each that she really was all right. And gradually they accepted it as truth and got up, each sighing deeply, as though they had also stopped breathing during the entire ordeal, and then each returned to the crowd, and then to the conversations that acknowledged them as participants in the drama. No one spoke to Hadad.

"Do you feel like standing up and getting out of the street?" he asked her.

Ruth laughed a little at herself. "I guess I am sort of holding up traffic, aren't I?"

The ambulance arrived just as Ruth was getting up.

"Don't let her move," the attendant shouted as he got out of the van.

Now the drama was repeated for the benefit of the late arrivals. Hadad stood back and watched as the emergency medical team went through its routines. There were others in the crowd eager to participate, to answer the questions about what had happened, to volunteer information for the reports made out in triplicate. It was hard for the person examining Ruth to accept that she could have endured the impact of the car and have no broken bones, no aches and pains to show for it. The driver, having gotten his reports filled out, came over to his companion and looked down at Ruth.

"Hey, Ruthie, sounds like you've been doing battle with a mechanical dragon. How's she doing, Frank? Is she going to live?"

"Mike, I can't find a scratch or a broken bone in her entire body. Seems a little farfetched to me."

"Aw, c'mon, Frank, you know Ruthie! She's not going to let us medical people get one up on her. A little hocus-pocus, a few herbs, and everything's okay, right, Ruthie?"

"Mike, I mean it. She's not faking it. She's okay."

"Well, let's take her in and put her under observation till she gets out of shock."

"Mike, she isn't in shock. Pulse is normal. Breathing regular. Body temperature regulated. Tell him how you feel, Ruth."

"Mike, I was about to get up and walk away when you got here. I'm okay."

"Still . . ."

"Okay, how about I come up and let you watch me for a while? Just don't make me ride in your hearse. I'll take my car."

"You shouldn't be driving."

"Okay, I'll get someone to drive me up. Okay?"

"What do you say, Frank?"

"Can't see any reason why not."

"Okay, but don't call it a hearse, you hear?"

Ruth grinned up at him and watched as he got to his feet, then pulled her up, slowly, cautiously, watching for any change in her balance or coloration. He seemed to accept that she was all right and the two men got back into the ambulance and hit the siren once, clearing the street in front of them, and then drove back up to the hospital, turning left at the corner.

Ruth found Hadad in the group on the sidewalk.

"I feel like somebody's fool. You let me go rambling on forever about all the healing I've done, but you never said a word about being a healer. Thank you."

"You said I owed you one."

"Accounts square. Thank you."

The eyes of the deer looked at Hadad once again. He stared back and then looked down at the sidewalk.

"Those grasses you eat," he said, trying to break the silence that he felt was far too public, "they are natural to you?"

"A lot of people think so."

"Other humans do not think so."

"No, I guess they don't. Why did you ask?"

"The energy returned rapidly. At home, I would have expected that. I was surprised."

"You've done this before?"

"It is part of my training . . ."

"I know . . . to be a king."

Hadad shrugged, a little embarrassed to be talking about his own skills.

The crowd, convinced that Ruth was able to walk again, aware that the excitement was over, began to move away. The driver got back into his car, moved it to the curb, and sat for a moment collecting himself.

And so Ruth and Hadad were left alone on the sidewalk. But not for long.

It started as a roar, like the sound of water rushing through a canyon in a flash flood—distant, unrelated, ominous, but unidentifiable.

And then they appeared. Running, four abreast, the red-uniformed Visitor soldiers rounded the corner of Main and Third, ignoring the "no left turn" sign, thundering down the street toward the courthouse. As they came, soldiers peeled away from the group in an orderly rhythm, their positions filled by the soldiers behind them, the smaller groups charging into the stores on either side of the street, the column running undaunted toward the goal.

There was still enough of a crowd to mobilize some resistance. A few braver ones ran toward the soldiers, trying to block their passage. Perhaps those few thought they would be killed for their efforts, but they were not. The soldiers did not fire, they just moved around them, not affected by their presence. No shots were fired. All the mobilization efforts outlined earlier seemed to disappear. The people stared open-mouthed, and their movements became random and chaotic, some trying to get out of the way, others trying to find shelter, others trying to protect the others on the street from something undefined, yet present. Others stood very still. Somewhere someone was screaming, but no one in the street screamed.

And then the Visitors climbed the steps of the courthouse and disappeared in the double doors and the old stone building swallowed them up. And suddenly, as quickly as it had begun, the invasion was complete. And once again there were no red-uniformed lizardmen on the streets. Now they were everywhere. And none were visible.

Hadad became aware that he was holding Ruth in his arms as he watched the parade. He was not certain why or how that had happened. He had not been aware of a moment when she had moved from the sidewalk in front of him, facing him, to face the invaders, nor of a moment when his arms had opened to surround her shoulders. But now she was there and he found he was holding her tightly to him.

There was a pause when the last uniform disappeared into the building. Anything could have happened in that moment. And nothing did. And then Hadad felt the quiet pulses in Ruth's body as she started to cry. He turned her around and looked into her eyes as she cried, still holding her close to him, and her crying stopped, and then her body calmed.

"Ruth, you do not have time to go to the hospital. I'm sorry. You must get out of town before they have control of all the roads. You must get to an airport. You must go to Los Angeles and find the resistance. They must dust the valley. You must convince them. Do you understand that?"

Ruth looked at him, about to cry again, but the tears did not come. His arms held her and again the tensions receded. She looked at him and this time the eyes of the deer held fear, but not of him. Slowly she nodded in acceptance of what she must do.

"I'll come back as soon as I can."

Hadad nodded. And then he let his arms drop to his sides.

She looked down at his hand and saw the bandage.

"Don't forget your medicine plant," she said, and smiled up at him.

"I won't."

"I'll come back."

Hadad recognized that she was saying more than

that she would return to Prineville, that somehow the return had something to do with him, something to do with doing what he had asked, but more. "Be careful."

"I will," she promised.

And then she took a breath, and turned away from him. Checking the highway, she crossed to her car. She got in, started it, and drove west, not looking back.

He watched her go. And realized he would not be there when she returned.

Chapter 6

Hadad woke well before dawn, as he had planned.

The night before he had wrapped his other clothes in a flannel shirt, tied the sleeves to secure the bundle, ground the leaves of the medicine plant, and mended his hand. His few tools and his eye drops were stashed in the pocket of his jacket along with his wallet. He left nothing behind.

Now he must remove his mark upon the space he had claimed.

One by one he took the stones back to the places they had occupied before he cleared them for his bed. With a branch he scored the land that had worn smooth with his daily squattings to watch the animals around him. He had brought water in a jar from Crooked River. He emptied the jar over the rocks where he had once stored his clothes. Then he gathered sage and juniper branches and ground them between rocks in each of the places he had imbued with his presence, with the scent of his occupancy.

He put on his jacket, picked up his bundle of clothes, and started down to the road.

The stars were completing their journey of the night. Cancer had dropped below the horizon; now Leo sat at the edge of the world and Scorpio ruled the southern sky. The Eagle, the Dolphin, and the Swan had just risen. The moon hid behind a solitary cloud on the rim of the plateau behind him. Hadad walked silently. He had eaten well before sleeping, knowing that he would have to travel today without food.

Knowing that he might not find food again that would
fill him without filling him with death.

There were no stirrings on Coombs Flat Road. A
light went on as he passed one house, an alarm clock
buzzed behind him in another. It would be a while yet
before even the early risers would emerge.

He reached the watch shed at the mill just as Dave
completed his last rounds of his shift.

"A bit early, aren't ya?"

"I am going west. I need an early beginning."

"Leavin' us, eh?"

Hadad looked evenly at Dave. He did not see
censure in the old man's question.

"Yes."

"Well, you're not alone. A good many started out
even yesterday. I'd probably go myself, but I just can't
figure where I'd go at my age. It's not like I can just
start up again anywhere. After a time you realize
you're gonna die somewhere. It doesn't much matter
where it is. And you might just as well be somewhere
you can call home when you do it. You young ones.
You've got a chance out there. I just hope there's still
somewhere out there that's safe for you to make a life
for yourselves."

"I hope so. I do not know."

"None of us know anything anymore."

"Some do not know that yet."

"They'll learn, or they'll die."

"You know that too?"

"You don't get to be as old as I am without learning
that somewhere along the line. That fella over there is
heading west. Maybe he'll give you a ride."

"Thank you, Dave."

"Luck to ya."

"To you also."

Hadad backed out of the watch shed. The old man

raised a hand as if to wave, and then turned back to his log sheet to record his rounds.

There was a blue pickup truck across the highway in the direction Dave had pointed. The man was adjusting a load of furniture and boxes, trying to add one additional box that just wouldn't fit without throwing the rest off balance. Hadad crossed the highway and swung a box out of the way to give a little assistance.

"Thanks." The man juggled his package into place and then adjusted the load so the others would fit.

"Dave, over there, says you are heading west."

"Soon as I fill the tank."

"Could I ride along?"

"Far as I'm going, sure. Could use the company to keep me awake. It's been a long night. You drive?"

"Sorry, no."

"No matter. As long as you keep talking."

"I will try."

"Name's Jerry." The man extended a hand.

"Dave." Hadad took the hand, watched the eyes.

"Hop in."

Hadad walked around to the curb, opened the door, stashed his bundle of clothes on the floor behind the seat, and then climbed up to the seat. As he closed the door, Jerry got in the driver's seat and started up. The truck pulled into Juniper Fuel and Stan came out from the office, shaking his head to clear the sleep that threatened to recapture him this early in the morning. He smelled of coffee as he stuck his head in the window of the cab.

"What'll it be, Jerry?"

"Fill 'er up, Stan. I'm headed back home."

"Looks like you've got a full load."

"Can't talk the folks into coming with me. They just loaded me up with stuff for the wife. You'd think . . ."

"Maybe they'll follow you when they see what happens."

"If they can. How about you, Stan?"

"Can't move Mary. Long as she's up there at the hospital, I'm stuck here. Soon as I can move her, I'm gone."

"Got anywhere to go?"

"Got family over in Eugene. Hey there, Dave. You headed out too?"

"Yes." Hadad nodded.

"Heard about what you did for Ruth yesterday. Wish you'd have been there when my Mary had her accident. Maybe she'd be up and walking now."

"What are you talking about?"

"Where you been, Jerry? Ruth got hit by a car yesterday. Dave here had her fixed up in just a couple minutes. Make him tell you about it."

"After you fill it up." He pointed over his shoulder with his thumb.

"Right on."

Hadad stared out at the dark road while the gas poured into the tank. He didn't want to volunteer. He wasn't certain his obligation to talk had started yet.

Jerry paid for the gas and started the truck up again. He drove carefully through town. A few cars were starting to move. Not many. The lights were still on at the courthouse, but there weren't any signs of life at the windows. The signal lights were all against them, and so they stopped at each, waited while nothing crossed their path, nothing approached them from behind, nothing met them from the front, and then as the light changed they moved to the next. Finally they reached the divided road at the end of town and started up the grade that would take them through Sisters and across the pass.

They rode in silence. After about ten miles Jerry

snapped on the radio. His taste ran to mellow country. Hadad listened to the words. In song after song the singers observed that love is not all it is cracked up to be, and life has its ups and downs, and basically people need each other to get through the troubles and to share the joys.

The sun came up in as ordinary a way as it can in the mountains. The shadows danced on the windshield as they drove through the forests, winding farther up, farther west.

In the middle of one song Jerry snapped off the radio.

"Can't stand that tune. What did Stan mean about you fixing Ruth up?"

"It was not difficult. She was hit by a car. There was no one there to do anything."

"First aid, you mean?"

"Everybody just looked at her and stood in a circle."

"Yeah, we're real good at circles in an emergency. Comes from our days out on the prairies with the Indians."

Hadad looked over at Jerry, looking for some clue to his statement. He found none. But in a moment Jerry looked over at him, tried to smile, got no encouragement, and gave up and looked back at the road.

"Sorry. Just trying to make a joke. The last couple hours have been more than I could handle. Go on, tell me about Ruth. What happened?"

"She ran across the street to her car without looking for the traffic. We had been talking. The car, it could not stop."

"So what did you do?"

"It was not special."

"Stan seemed to think it was. He said something about if you'd been there when Mary was hurt. That's special as far as he's concerned. What did ya do? Come on, man, spill. Ruth's a friend of mine. I'm interested."

"She has told you about her healing, then?"

"More than told me. Every time I see her she's trying to convert me to something. She got you converted?"

"No."

"Got you're own special magic, eh?"

Hadad laughed at that. Not a lot. Just a little. The man would not let him keep his silence. He thought about what he could say that would answer the question. They came around the bend and sharply etched before them were the jagged edges of yet a higher mountain. And then the turn took them beyond it, and another turn took it from view.

"Hurt is jagged like that mountain. Healing is putting the jagged pieces back inside instead of sticking out all over. Earth ones are smooth when they aren't hurt or aren't angry, or frightened."

"Earth ones, eh? Sounds like you're from outer space."

"What would you say?"

"People."

"But animals are the same way."

"I get your point. Just sounds funny, 'Earth ones!' I mean, you're an Earth one too. Do you say that about yourself?"

"No." Hadad was honest, but he said nothing more.

"Sorry, I didn't mean to criticize. You talk like you're from somewhere else."

"I learned American second."

"What did you learn first?"

"I don't know your word for it."

"Where are you from?"

"I was to be in Pau, to build the city again in the desert."

"Never heard of it."

"It is a lost city."

"Like Atlantis."

"What is Atlantis?"

"We're back where we started from, a lost city."

"Then, yes, like Atlantis."

"I give up. Where did you learn to do healing?"

"At home."

"In Pau."

"No. At home."

"Oh."

Hadad looked at Jerry. The man was trying so hard to start a conversation, and Hadad felt he'd broken his commitment to talk, and so he looked for words, something that would do more than just answer the questions.

"Where I used to live, my people, we all do healing. It isn't a special thing with us. That's not true with all of my people. But it is true of all of us who are the marked people."

"Like the mark of Cain?"

"I do not know about the mark of Cain."

"Just talk, forget my comparisons. They don't matter anyway."

"Ruth broke her leg."

"And you healed a broken leg, just like that, right there on the spot?"

"She is very healthy."

"Is that all it takes, to be very healthy?"

"It helps."

"You're beyond me. I thought Ruth was way out there, but she's never cured a broken leg."

Hadad became concerned that he had made too much of the healing. He did not want Jerry to think he was different, foreign, someone to suspect. He changed the subject.

"Your parents are still in Prineville?"

"They won't leave."

"They must leave."

"They say there's nowhere else that's safer."

"That is not true."

"Tell *them* that. I already know it."

Jerry turned on the radio again and Hadad took that as a signal that his services as talker were no longer needed.

After a few songs Jerry snapped the radio off again.

They rode for more than an hour in silence.

"Where are you going?" Jerry asked abruptly.

"Away from Prineville," Hadad answered simply; but then he went on, trying to understand, to meet the abruptness of the question. "I had to leave Prineville. I am not a brave man. I do not have to defend a home. I have no family here."

"I'm not questioning your loyalties. I'm just wondering where you're going. I'm stopping up here a way and I suddenly don't know what to do with you. Where do you want me to let you off?"

"This place will do as well as any other. Death will find me wherever I am. Life is as good here as anywhere."

"Es la vita."

Hadad looked at the sign that marked the village they were entering. He read, "Vida," and assumed the expression Jerry had voiced referred to the town. He looked around. Civilization stretched along the road. Nut orchards measured the yards to the river, houses nestled in the clearings in the narrow stretches beneath the sharp rise of forested mountains. The river ran swiftly, making a turn as it reached a covered bridge and then, slowing into stillness beyond the bridge, reflecting the almost cloudless sky.

"Seriously, Dave. Are you telling me you don't have anywhere to go?"

"Jerry, I am running away. I am not running to. This will serve me as well as anywhere else. I appreciate your ride."

"Hell, man, come home with me then. There's always room for one more."

"I could not . . ."

"Man, where do you think you're going to live? This is a small community. You either know someone, or you buy a home. There's no work here, no hotels. You're coming home with me. I'm not going to just let you wander off into the forest. Come on."

Jerry pulled into his driveway, got out, and started unloading the truckbed. There was nothing for Hadad to do but to help. It would have been rude to leave him there with all the boxes and furniture to carry. And so Hadad carried as he had at the mill.

There was family. Jerry had a wife, Madge; a son, Tony. The only concern at first was where were the parents. And then when the questions were answered there were introductions. Hadad was welcomed and another place was set at the table and he was shown to a room that he could sleep in, and then Madge began to cook the major meal of the day. It was still morning. Hadad had not been in a home in which cooking was the major function, and so he was puzzled at all the preparations. And he was not a part of all the conversations that accompanied the work.

He went outside and browsed the edge of the farm. He saw mice. He watched. He was not hungry yet. He was hungry, but not hungry enough to take a chance yet on what he ate. He watched the mice and wondered if they carried the virus. Soon he would have to take the chance. He waited, watching, wondering if he had come to Vida to die.

"There you are. Dinner's almost ready. Come on in and eat."

"I cannot."

"Dave, you're welcome here. You're not imposing. I could use some help on the farm if you need work. It's okay."

"I cannot eat."

Jerry came over and squatted beside him. He did not say anything more. After a while Jerry watched the mice too.

"I gather there's something bothering you, something more than your welcome."

Hadad didn't answer.

"Look, Dave, a lot of people are going to be uprooted in this. It's that or die. You're lucky you don't have anyone to leave behind or take with you."

Hadad looked at him and then back down at the mouse that was peeking out from the clutter of tools and toys.

"Wrong again, eh? There is someone. Someone back in Prineville. Are you sure you were right to leave?"

Hadad nodded.

"That's a tough one. Did you have to leave her there?"

Hadad didn't respond.

"Or wouldn't she come?"

Hadad looked at Jerry. He didn't say anything or suggest anything. He just looked.

"Trouble between you, eh?"

Hadad looked back at the mouse.

"Look, I'm not one to give advice, I don't know you. I don't know her. You have to make your own decisions in life. But when you care about someone, it's hard when you can't agree. I don't know what to say. You're welcome here. Maybe she'll change her mind. Look, come on in and have some dinner. Maybe you'll feel better if you eat something."

"I cannot eat."

"At least come inside."

"You and Madge are happy."

"Yes; yes, we are. . . . Oh, I see. That does make it rough, doesn't it? I've been there. It's hard to be around happiness when you're not happy. I got it. What are you going to do?"

Hadad looked up toward the forest.

"You can probably camp out there. They're not cutting at the moment. I doubt anyone would hassle you at this point. You can tell them you're my guest if it helps."

Hadad nodded.

"Let me at least fix you up with a tent and a sleeping bag. We've got a whole bunch of gear. You might as well be comfortable out there if you won't stay here."

He left and rummaged in the storage shed behind the house and came back with a tent, a sleeping bag, a lantern, and a canvas bag with straps that seemed to be stuffed with odd-shaped angular items.

"Here, this should get you started. Come back if you need anything else. I tossed in some freeze-dried food in case you change your mind about eating. And there's a canteen of water in there too. And matches. Anything else you need, come on back. And don't worry about them. Just drop them by when you're done with them."

Hadad nodded.

"And, Dave, I mean it; if there's anything—" Jerry stopped, and went back to the house.

Hadad looked at the camping equipment. There was nothing he could use. But if he didn't take it,

Jerry would be suspicious. He left the pile on the ground, went back to the truck for his clothes, came back to get the gear, and then headed uphill behind the farm into the reforested stand of trees that reached straight up behind the house.

The forest was damp. Hadad found a spot close to the ridge, a spot clear enough to make a dugout unnoticed from the road below, sheltered from anyone hovering above, yet open enough to give him a vantage point over Vida and the highway. He dug with his feet, not randomly as a dog will dig, but measuredly carving a space that would fit him, give him a space to store, and no more.

The ground was damp, and the rocks he uncovered were cold. It was not like the desert. The temperature was warmer but the chill was colder. He tried to lie on the ground and found the moisture crept into his clothes.

Among the items in the canvas pack was a square of heavy plastic. It was smudged with paint, dusty with red clay, but untorn. Hadad fit the plastic into the hovel, edged it with stones, burying the edges to keep them down. The rest of the gear he put in the storage place behind a rock with the other clothes he had carried.

He worked and then he watched.

He did not look for food.

The day moved slowly through the trees. Gradually it was replaced by woodsmoke. And then there were stars.

He was watched that night by the forest dwellers. He sat and established his presence. At dawn, he gave in to sleep.

The next day he made his peace with life and started to look for food. There were strange ratlike creatures with sharp teeth that were easy to catch by their tails. The smaller ones were tender, the larger ones chewed like leather. It was easy to find insects to season the food, but for the most part they were scrawny specimens, all crackle and little meat.

He did not die.

He waited for death for days, but he did not die.

And so he began to seek life and to become a part of the community below him. There was some work at Rhodoland. At night he swept the floors at Ike's Pizza. When people asked where he lived, he said he was Jerry's guest, and that seemed to satisfy everyone. He found that people wanted to talk. There weren't many places to go, and so people talked to one another, more than the people in Prineville had. He learned that the rush of the river told the men of Vida about the weather around them, beyond their valley. He learned the language of the filbert crop from the man at Filacres, the talk of the real estate people who were drawing in the "other" people up Goodpasture Road —people who were not farmers, had not grown up in the narrow gorge, but who had come looking for a hideaway in the Oregon mountains. He listened, and became part of the backdrop of Vida, just as he had become part of the backdrop of Prineville. In time, the townspeople greeted him by name. And none ever realized that he had become accepted as one of them without ever revealing who he was or anything about himself.

He purchased a plastic ground cover to replace the one that he had taken from the canvas pack. And he bought another jacket, one like the men in Vida wore, one that withstood the rain and looked of the mountains.

When he was part of the mountain as well as part of the town, he packed up the gear to return it to Jerry.

He swung the pack over his shoulder and lifted the

tent before he saw her standing watching him. It upset him that anyone had been able to watch him without his knowing it. He looked back over the moments to calculate when he had abandoned his awareness of the road, of the forest, of the sounds of movement. He found the last moment of recall and worked forward, realizing he had been absorbed in the repacking of the gear, as an Earth one would be.

Ruth stood a little below him on the trail he would take back to Jerry's farm. He could see her old car below her on Angel's Flight Road. She watched him. He stopped his movements and stared back at her. She looked down at the ground and then back at him. She looked as if she expected him to say something. He walked toward her and stopped just in front of her.

"I wasn't certain I'd find you."

"Why are you here?"

"You weren't there when I got back."

"But why are you here?"

"You send me off on a wild goose chase to a city that doesn't even look like it used to, to find people whose names I don't even know, who don't know I'm coming or whether to trust me or not, carrying a message that I can't confirm or explain, telling me to be sure not to tell the wrong people when I don't even know who the right people are, let alone who the wrong people are, driving off in the middle of nowhere to catch a plane with money I haven't got, all because of some blamed theory of yours, and then when I get back you aren't even there to ask me if I did what you said."

"You did what I said?"

"Yes."

"And they have sent the red dust to Prineville?"

"No."

"No?"

"They wouldn't do it. They told me that if they use any more red dust anywhere, the ecology will be thrown off balance. Apparently the rest of us can withstand only so much of the stuff in our systems before we get sick from it too."

"But there is no red dust in Prineville."

"I told them that, but they didn't believe me. Or maybe they believed me. They just wouldn't do anything about it."

"And you told the right people?"

"As far as I know. Look, I don't know. I may have told the only spies they have in the resistance. Maybe I got the wrong people, the wrong answers. I did the best I could under the circumstances."

"And you went back to Prineville?"

"I went back to find you."

"And it was safe for you in Prineville?"

"It's not safe for anyone in Prineville. It's just like you said it would be. The Visitors have taken over. They are taking people, no one knows where. People disappear. There is resistance. Everyone shoots first and asks questions later. It's hard to tell what is more dangerous, waiting to be taken by the Visitors, or trying to drive through the town and find the resistance. There aren't any windows left that aren't broken. It's like a ghost town with the skeletons still fighting the war. Nobody trusts anyone else. It's horrible. No one can save Prineville now."

"We must tell Jerry. His parents are still there."

"I told him. He left an hour ago to get them."

"It will not be safe for him to drive there."

"He's already gone."

"He will need help."

"Hadad, he's already gone."

He looked at her and realized that he had not seen

the look on her face that he had seen before. He turned his head and looked more closely at her face. She closed her eyes and looked down at the ground by her feet.

"How did you find me here?"

"I went to the mill. It was the only place I could think of to look. They didn't know anything. Mary told me Stan knew where you were, or at least that he'd seen you before you left. I'd given up hope of finding you by then. I was just working up at the hospital, trying to keep people alive, to do something."

"But you do not run away. Why did you come here?"

"Because you are here, not there."

"To give me the message then?"

"It doesn't matter what the message is if you're not there. You knew what would happen. It happened."

"And you are here."

"Yes."

Hadad looked again at the eyes that looked at him. This time he saw "the deer," but also he saw sadness.

"I do not understand."

"I am here to find you."

"And you have found me."

Hadad watched as she shook her head.

"Maybe I . . . I . . . I want to be where you are."

"But I am here on the mountain."

"Then I want to be here on the mountain."

"But you do not live as I do."

"Then I will live as you do."

"But you cannot."

"You haven't even given me a chance."

"That is not what I mean. I have no things to make you comfortable here. I . . ."

He looked again at the face, at the eyes, at the

sadness, and he was confused. He still carried the things he was taking back to Jerry. He still stood in the path where he had encountered her. He did not want to take her to the place where he slept, to the place where he watched the animals, to the place that was his ground. He chose instead a place higher on the mountain, where the old trees were. He turned to go there.

"Come."

She followed.

They climbed up through the young timbers, climbed as a deer would climb without a path. The edge of the old trees was rougher. There the undergrowth had been cut, but never cleared. They had to pick their way through vines and ferns. And rocks were stubborn in their ways—loose when footing was needed, and firm when they were blocking the way.

There was a copse that Hadad knew. He had been there often, choosing it as a place to sit and work with his tools. There he would work the stone, the wood, the metals he found, into shapes that were useful, or interesting to the eye.

He entered the cluster of trees and she followed. Here he could put down the gear he had been carrying. Here he could put down the confusion that he did not know how to carry.

They sat on a fallen tree.

"Tell me in different words why you are here."

Ruth looked at the ground, pushed a path with the toe of her boot, and then looked directly at him.

"I think I love you very deeply."

Hadad looked at the eyes and knew then what he saw there.

"And there is nowhere else for you to go?"

"There is nowhere else I want to go."

He felt the pull to move toward her, the way he had

felt it in Prineville before the car, before she had left the curb. He knew now what that pulling was and now he resisted it.

"Ruth, you cannot stay here."

"I have a tent and everything I need, everything we need."

"We cannot stay on this mountain. And it is all I have."

"Jerry said we can stay on his farm. I asked."

"You cannot stay with me."

"I don't believe that. I don't believe for one minute that you want me to go away. Please don't make me beg."

"Ruth, we are different."

"Hadad, I don't know anything about the ways of your people, and the ways of my people don't apply right now. I don't know how to say what I'm saying. I don't know how to let you know what I know. But my heart says that I'm not wrong to be here. I look in your eyes and know that you feel what I feel. I won't accept your words that say we can't be together, because there isn't any logic in them. We *can* be together, and my truth inside says you want that as much as I do. I don't know why you hold back. I don't know why you force the distance between us. But I do know the distance is a lie. And I haven't got time for lies. My world is collapsing around me. I haven't got time to wait for you to come to the truth in your own way. I love you. And I want to spend whatever time we have left on this planet with you. And nothing else matters very much."

"You see only what is on the outside."

"It's not the outside I'm looking at. I didn't fall in love with you for your looks. Your hair's too coarse, your nose is too big, your hands are larger than your face, your musculature is all wrong, and your eyes are glassy and hide the truth. I'd never paint you as a hero. What I see is on the inside. What I love is on the inside."

"And what you do not see is between the two."

"You think you are so different because what you feel and what you think are not the same. You think you are so different because you don't belong to this culture. But we're all in this together. We struggle along trying to carve out a little happiness for ourselves wherever we can. I may not know the secrets you think you're hiding from me, but whatever they are, I'll face them. I can't argue with what you say I don't know about you. But I can say this: What I do know about you is that you are honest and kind. And I can't believe there is anything about you that puts a lie to that."

"I cannot argue to convince you. I can only say it will not work."

"Then you will have to tell me you do not love me."

Hadad looked at her. She did not hide behind her eyes. She did not hide in a glance away from his face. She did not hide in a binding look. She waited. He did not look away.

"I cannot tell you that."

"Then there is no argument that will make me go away."

"There is one."

"I don't believe you."

"I have come to the mountain to die."

"Then I will observe your death."

"I am running away."

"Then I will help you."

"I have no home."

"Then we will make one."

"I am not who you think I am."

"Then I will learn who you are."

"And then you will leave."

"I have no reason to leave."

Hadad looked at her and knew he must send her away. She had a world to travel, to heal, to rescue. He wanted to hold her and knew he could not live a lie.

"Ruth, I am a Visitor."

Chapter 7

"There aren't any arguments that will convince me, Hadad." Her response came in the same rhythm as the ones before.

Hadad watched her, waiting.

"Call it arrogance, if you like, but I'm not afraid of the differences between us."

Hadad watched. Still she carried the energy of her own argument without hearing the truth in his.

"I don't . . ." The words failed her, and then the tears came. She sat just as she had before; her body did not respond. But her eyes closed and her face contorted. When she opened her eyes, they were soft-focused, wet, and faintly accusing.

"It's not fair."

"It is the truth."

"But you told me to—"

"What is not fair is for my people to take advantage of your people. That is not fair."

"But what about—"

"Ruth, I will live on the mountain until I die."

"No, no, no, no!" She shook her head violently from side to side and the tears now flowed freely, the sobs grabbing at her torso. Hadad reached out to calm her.

"Don't touch me! Don't . . . Don't . . ." She pulled away from him and, shaking her head back and forth in a frenzy, got to her feet and backed away out of the clearing and then ran down the mountainside.

Hadad sat very still, waiting with the rest of the forest for the thunder of human catastrophe to pass.

He heard her cries all the way down the mountain. He heard her steps, at one point sure, at another faulty, then sureness regained, then another stumble. At one point she tripped and fell. The sobs continued. She got up and went on. And then she reached her car, and he heard the metal and then the ignition and the roar of the engine and the high-pitched whine of the brakes, and then the rush of departure, hanging in the air for minutes while the car navigated the curves of the road heading west.

The forest waited in the stillness.

Hadad waited for the forest.

A field mouse ran across the log where Ruth had been sitting.

Hadad watched, without moving, without wanting to move. The mouse investigated the log and went on. And then in another moment a jay overhead mocked him for his foolishness. Gradually the sounds returned to fill the clearing.

A piece of wood lay at Hadad's feet. He reached for it and turned it over and over in his hands. He recognized in the grain the flow of hair, and so he took his knife from his pocket and began the slow, careful process of delineating features, evoking the texture of a face, rounding the crown for a head, sculpting the smooth line of a neck and the spread of bare shoulders. There the wood stopped, and so he returned to the face to work it further into expression and personality.

He had worked for hours before he realized that the face he was carving was Ruth's. It bothered him to look at it. And yet he could not destroy the work, nor discard it. Now started, he felt compelled to finish it and to refine the work so that it was even more a resemblance.

He would not take food here in this place. This was a place of sharing, of stillness. And so when the sun had shifted to the west and he became aware of the hours passing, he began to think of going down the mountain to hunt. He had not eaten all day, and even now he did not feel hungry. He was not comfortable with the longing he felt. And it was disquieting to realize he had now told someone who he was. He had been safe as long as no one knew. Now he must always be alert.

He put the knife into his pocket and the carving on the log beside him, picked up the camping gear and returned to the side of the mountain where he slept. He left the gear there and wandered east, seeking the canyons beyond that were shadowed now and would be alive with rodents seeking food themselves. He covered several miles before he was satisfied. Mice, crickets, shrews, a cardinal, two squirrels, four beetles, and a handful of ants made him feel better. But there was still the gnawing feeling of discontent, of longing, that food would not satisfy.

He returned to the cave and picked up the gear. He would return it to Jerry, find out if Jerry's parents were safe, and then return to the mountain to sleep. He longed for sleep to exorcise the growing anxiety, the feeling of emptiness, of pointlessness, of impatience.

The truck was up by the house half full of packages, the tarp that had covered them pulled back but not removed. Jerry came out from the house, reached for another bundle, and did not see Hadad emerging from the forest. He returned to the house, and when he came back, Hadad was by the truck taking out yet another box.

"Thanks. I can use your help."

"You found them all right."

"I found them. My dad had been shot. Just surface wounds, but he's in a lot of pain. Mom's frightened. I had to sneak them out of town under the tarp. Dave, it's bad. The town reeks of rotting meat. Everything's boarded up. There's nothing left. A few people hiding in closets. I brought a neighbor, an old lady the folks have been hiding. There's nothing left."

"You had trouble to get into town?"

"Ruth brought me a pass to get me through the roadblock. She'd taken it off a dead body up at the hospital. That got me in. It was harder getting out. They search everything. Had to go north, cross a few ranches. Ended up on a firebreak. That got me back to the highway above the roadblock. It wasn't a very comfortable ride in back here. But I guess it was better than getting dead."

"It is almost over, then, in Prineville."

"Probably in Prineville. But they won't stop there. They'll spread out, get the other communities in the valley, and then start up the mountains. It's only a matter of time before they come here. We'll give the folks a few weeks to recuperate, and then we're heading north. It's funny, Dave. No place is safe. You look at the face of one of those aliens and you see everything you've ever seen in another man: hopes, fears, dreams, plans, maybe even love. But they're rotten inside. You can't trust any of them."

"What about the fifth column?"

"They're only pretending to help the resistance. They've got their own motives. I wouldn't trust 'em. We're stuck with running, man. There isn't any solution. All we can hope is that we can kill off the ones who find us and run from those who haven't caught up with us yet."

"I take this in for you."

"Thanks. You can meet the folks."

Hadad had picked up the largest of the boxes, expecting it to be the heaviest, and found it awkwardly light. It took both arms to balance it, and he had trouble seeing around it to the steps and so he maneuvered sideways. He backed into the house, being careful not to scrape his knuckles on the door-jamb. The boxes were stacked on the far side of the living room by the archway. He crossed the room and added this one to the stack. He then turned, saw Madge, nodded in greeting, and then saw the three elderly people huddled on the couch, wrapped in blankets, each holding a steaming mug, staring at him, unsmiling.

Jerry came in with a laundry basket, put it by the door, and started the introductions.

"Dave, this is my mother and father, Evelyn and Ralph, and this is Mrs. Hardesty. I told you, Mother. Dave is from Prineville, used to work at the mill. I brought him up here my last trip."

The woman Jerry had indicated was his mother nodded politely, even tried to smile, but the weariness from the trip made it a feeble attempt. The man nodded automatically, starting to doze again, obviously awakened by the intrusion, unwilling to attend to anything more than the steaming liquid he was holding, almost unable to stay awake long enough to enjoy it.

Mrs. Hardesty was older than the others, wizened and gnarled, but alert and cautious. She looked him over carefully and then rose from her seat, bent and crippled, and walked cautiously toward him. She sniffed at him and looked him over again. She growled before she spoke. The sound came from her throat, but its anger came from deeper.

"Get out of here. You're one of *them*. Get out of here and leave us alone." Her voice was gravelly but distinct. And her eyes pierced any illusion that she was senile. "Jerry, get this alien out of this house immediately. You've brought one of them here. Now none of us are safe."

Hadad froze, staring at the old woman. She was the

first human he had met with the senses of an animal. She did not frighten him; she had no power except, perhaps, the power to influence. But he respected the keenness of her perceptions and knew she would never be swayed by any argument in his favor.

"Mrs. Hardesty, this is my friend."

"You're a fool. He's got you fooled. I can smell it in him. Get him out of here. Get us away from him."

Hadad looked over to Jerry, and then, embarrassed, looked at the floor. He glanced up at Madge, saw her embarrassment, tried to smile, and nodded, and then went to the door and out to the porch. Jerry followed him.

"Dave, I apologize. What can I say? After what they've been through, she has to be scared of her own shadow. I can't blame her, but I'm sorry she took it out on you."

Hadad nodded and went around the bed of the truck to get the gear he had brought back.

"I have finished."

"This doesn't mean you're leaving us, does it?"

"No, just I have finished."

"Ruth found you then."

"You knew she was looking for me?"

"Look, buddy, I don't mean to presume, but from the look on her face when she asked about you, I sort of put two and two together. There's room out behind the shed for a tent; Tony has had one up there every summer. I'll keep Mrs. Hardesty out of your hair. You won't bother us. You're welcome to stay."

"Ruth has gone away."

"Her choice or yours?"

"Jerry, it is not right for her to come here."

"Dave, she hasn't got anywhere else to go either. Territory gets shifted under conditions like these. She's welcome."

"But I cannot be for her."

"She's not the one?"

"I do not understand 'not the one.' "

"She's not the girl you left in Prineville?"

"She was in Prineville, yes."

"Dave, maybe I'm sticking my nose in where it doesn't belong, but I don't see any reason when two people love each other why they don't give it try. What can it hurt? If it doesn't work out, she goes away, that I can understand. But I think you're crazy letting her go when you feel the way you do."

"And how do I feel?"

"You mean you don't care about her?"

"Jerry, I am committed to Ruth's happiness."

"Yeah."

"She is strong. She will endure. She is entitled to have happiness. She will find someone who can be for her."

"And you? What about you, Dave? Are you strong? Will you endure? Are you entitled to happiness? Will you find someone who can 'be' for you?"

"There is no one who can be for me."

"That's hogwash, man. You've just been alone too long. You've forgotten what it feels like to be loved. You're a fool, man. I say go find her; bring her back."

"To use your words, I love her. And so I tell her I cannot be for her."

"You're crazy, Dave."

"Perhaps to you."

"Perhaps to me. If you change your mind, there's always room."

Jerry took another basket into the house. Hadad saw the mattress in the bed of the truck and lifted it onto the porch. He did not attempt to go inside with it. Jerry did not come out right away, and so Hadad left the camping gear on the porch as well, and went back across the garden and off into the woods.

It was twilight in the gorge. The sky above was still

blue, and the pines etched a sharp silhouette at the top of the ridge. Soft grays replaced the vivid tones of daylight, woodsmoke augmented the damp green of evening. The moon was high, still pearlescent in the light-blue sky.

Hadad climbed diligently, wearied by the day, eager for sleep, unwilling to break the rhythm of the forest by hurrying. He moved above his cave, broke the pattern of his climb, and came back by a different route, as he always did. He was not followed by man. Man would stalk him. Man he must outrun. He was not followed this time by dog or coyote. But at other times they had followed. And so he changed his patterns continually to keep his private places separate from the eyes of predators.

He expected to find his space unnoticed, undisturbed. He had never found animals inspecting it, having edged his space, his territory, with rue. And so he was ready for the sleep to come when he came into the clearing.

She was seated on the pallet he had made of worn blankets, and at first she looked down at the figure she was tracing on the cloth in front of her, but as he stepped into the clearing, Ruth looked up and stared at him, penetrating him with the searching eyes of the deer, binding him with unblinking eyes that pulled him toward her, this time without restraint, without condition, without reservation.

He moved toward her without question, and knelt beside her, searching her face for tears, for anger, finding none. She was wearing a leather garment that fell around her like a tent, only places for head and arms piercing it. As he watched she reached for the bottom edge of the leather and pulled it up over her head. And when the garment cleared her hair and was laid aside, she sat fully unclothed, unguarded, her eyes still on his, still unguarded. She unfolded her legs and stretched out on the pallet, trembling just slightly, never taking her eyes from his, still pulling him toward her with the look. He stretched over her and leaned down to kiss her, calming her with his touch, warming with the contact of her skin, embracing her at last.

With ease he pushed himself up from her and looked at her body. She was smooth and gaunt, small breasts almost flattened to her rib cage as she lay on her back, her stomach mounded slightly between heavy-boned hips, and light-brown hair lay in small curls in the triangle above her long thin legs. He pulled his weight back from his arms and took off the shirt and pants that bound him now. He longed to touch her without the plastic human disguise between their bodies. He looked back to her face and again her eyes drew him down to her. Carefully he kissed her, keeping his tongue concealed behind his lips, excitement concealed behind his contact lenses. He knew she could not see the natural color of his eyes shift as he moved his body to her. But he could not conceal his desire and she did not conceal hers. Now there were no differences that mattered. And the earth, hard beneath them, did not care.

The forest cooled gradually as the ground gave up the daywarmth. Bats and swallows took to the air to feast on insects, an owl waked and crossed the clearing. Squirrels chattered from the branches above. The sun abandoned the sky, and the moon, no longer in competition, lighted the forest for the night creatures.

Hadad pulled a layer of blanket from beneath them to wrap Ruth, concerned that her body heat might dissipate in the night air. His own temperature had dropped to match the air around him. He hesitated to touch her face now that his hands were cold, and settled for stroking her hair.

In a few moments Ruth opened her eyes and looked up at him. Now there was no pull, no hunger. He leaned down to kiss her.

Again his body pressed to hers beneath the light blanket.

"You're cold."

"Yes, do you mind?"

"What a silly question. Here, get more of the blanket."

"That will not warm me. The blanket warms you with the heat of your own body. But I do not feel cold."

"Oh."

"There are differences. . . . You came back."

"I'm still not certain I believe you." She looked up into his eyes, frightened, almost crying.

"Ruth, you must believe me. I cannot lie to you."

"That I do believe. You don't . . . feel different."

"Except the cold."

"That's not what I meant."

"I know. Our anatomy is very parallel to yours. That is why The Leader styled the invasion of Earth as he did. It was easy for us to look as you do. The differences are internal. And some are subtle."

"You say 'The Leader' the same way that—"

"He is The Leader."

"But he's done such horrible things to Earth, to all of us."

"Because he has considered you less than lizard. You are sentient beings, but you have such primitive belief and scientific systems that he could not pretend that your life form was important in the grander scale. I have read your history books in the library where I learned American. You have done the same things."

"But we didn't eat human beings."

"No, not all of you eat human beings. But some of you do eat lizards."

Hadad laughed and Ruth hesitantly laughed with him.

He quieted and looked at her eyes, looking for the question that could be answered that would take the fear from her body. She was tense beside him, withdrawn though very present.

"Are you certain you want to be here on the mountain with me?"

She nodded.

"It will not be easy. I do not live as you live. You will have to teach me how to make it comfortable for you to be with me. I have always lived alone, even with my family."

"Me too."

Hadad reached beyond her and took the leather garment she had been wearing and placed it over the blanket that covered her. He stretched out on his back and looked up at the sky through the tall trees. There were clouds. He had dug the shelter deep enough to keep him from the rain as he slept alone. If it rained tonight, he would get wet. He would have to reconsider all of this in the morning. Now he wondered how to sleep. Always he faced out onto the mountain, aware even in sleep of all the movement around him in the night. To sleep that way tonight he must turn his back to Ruth, and he wanted now to hold her to him, feel her warmth against his chest. He turned toward her, pulling her toward him, toward sleep. And for a few hours he was content and she was still. But with the late coyote call he waked, uncomfortable, sensing the world behind him.

He wanted to move, but he did not want to waken her. He looked at her hair, curled on her arm tucked under her head. As he watched her, she turned and moved a bit away from him. And then, content that she was comfortable, he turned to face out into the night.

It rained at dawn. Light drops touched his face, then began to dampen the blanket that covered him. He got up carefully and tucked the blanket around Ruth, folding it back away from the edge so that it did not catch the moisture and draw it back to her sleeping body. He found his clothes where he had discarded them the night before and dressed quietly. He was hungry and there would be early stirrings in the rodent world that would make a nice breakfast.

Ruth was awake when he returned. She wore the leather garment and had straightened the blankets into the pallet as she had found it the day before. The rain had stopped and now she sat cross-legged as she had been when he had come upon her before. But this time her eyes were closed and her arms outstretched on her knees. There was an acrid smell from the trees below the cave.

Hadad approached quietly and then crouched on the ground beside her, looking out through the cut in the trees, down to the river below. The sun danced on the rapidly moving water.

"Good morning. You sure get up early."

"Often. But not always."

"This morning, I . . ."

He looked over at her and saw her head bowed, her hair hanging forward over her face. She rubbed her nose with the back of her hand.

"You have been sick."

"Yes."

"I wasn't asking. I know."

"It happens. In the morning."

"That is because of the life you are carrying. Your body is discarding all that it does not need for that life and your own."

Ruth's head snapped up at him and her eyes glared. She searched his face, and then sharply looked away, back to her hands as they fiddled with the blanket folds in front of her.

"I felt the life in you last night. It is not a forbidden thing for my people. Earth ones are different. But I did not sense that you . . . The father, he is in Prineville?"

Ruth shook her head.

"Dead?"

"As good as."

"I'm sorry, Ruth. I wish I could bring him back for you, but the process of revitalization is complex and would require the help of my people and they would not do that for me. I will guard his child and you. That is all I can do for him now."

Ruth sighed. "No, Hadad, he's not on the ship. It's not that."

"What then?"

"It just didn't work. He doesn't know I'm pregnant. I'd rather he didn't."

"He does not be with you?"

"That's about it, he does not be with me."

"I am sorry."

"I used to think I was. I'm not anymore. I'd rather be with you."

"Maybe someday you will say that is not anymore."

"Hadad, please don't."

He looked at her and saw the sadness in her eyes that would not go away. He wanted to see her smile, and so he smiled, and as the first ray of sun broke through the trees to light her face, she smiled back and reached toward him to kiss him.

The cave was too small to give them both comfort. But Ruth had camping equipment in the car. There was no room for her tent in the small clearing on the side of the mountain, but there was room in the copse where they had talked. The older trees would give them more cover from passersby on the highway below. They could not watch Vida so closely, but that was foresaken for other pleasures. They carried the bundles up from the car and began to raise the tent.

The northeast corner was staked just beside the log where Ruth had been sitting the day before. She glanced at the log and saw there a small chunk of wood with her own likeness carved carefully into the grain.

"Hadad, what is this?"

There was one last tap on the other stake and he came around from the other side of the tent to see what she was looking at. He found her turning the sculpture over and over in her hands.

"I did not know what I was seeing in the wood when I started."

"It's good."

"Thank you."

"May I have it?"

"Yes."

She put it inside the tent and went back to drawing the fabric taut with the stake.

When they had brought all of Ruth's things from the car, Hadad left for town. It was time for him to sweep at the pizza parlor. He left without explanation.

The restaurant was empty when he arrived. Only the kitchen door was open. It would be another hour before the ovens were heated for the day. He took the broom and started among the tables, sweeping first, readying the floor to mop it later. A chair or two were still on the floor; he turned them up on the tables like the others. He thought of Ruth as he swept. And when his broom hit the table leg, he realized that he had finished half the floor without the attention he usually gave it. He shook his head and put aside his thoughts and focused on the floor. He swept. He mopped. He set chairs. And he thought of nothing else.

Ruth was angry when he returned. He did not understand why. She could not find the words to explain. He watched her angry. And then the anger was gone. It was late and she was tired and so they slept, wrapped together under the heavier blankets in the tent. He slept happily with her in his arms for a while, and then, as she had the night before, she turned, and he turned away from her, but there was only the side of the nylon tent. He could not see out into the night. He listened for a while to the night creatures moving in the area around the tent. And then he closed his awareness and fell into a restless sleep.

He awoke with the first stirrings of the jay in the tree above, and went out to find food.

He went back to his cave, having eaten, and expected to find his fresh clothes behind the rocks where he had left them. They were not there. For a moment he was disoriented, and then he realized that Ruth must have taken them. And then he was upset. He went back to the upper clearing and hunted through the draped materials strung on the line beside the tent. He found his clothes and changed into them. When Ruth came out from the tent, he looked at her, still angry, and then he dropped his head, aware that she would not understand that she had offended him.

He looked up again and smiled and when she smiled at him he felt her calling him with her eyes, pulling him back into the tent and back to her arms. He did not resist.

It was never easy. He felt the closeness of the old trees, the confinement of the tent, the preoccupation with "things" annoying. She complained of his long absences, his sudden disappearances, his preoccupation with the sounds of the forest around them.

They went to town. The people accepted Ruth, first as Jerry's friend, familiar from previous visits, now as Hadad's companion. For a while it was easier to be together with other people around to filter the differences. But the tension from the desert was pressing too close.

There had been hover craft sighted upriver, and the hostility of the people of Vida for the Visitors became more evident. Their blame was categorical and everyone was expected to share the opinion. Hadad was used to the accusations that he knew did not include him as long as his identity was hidden; would include him if ever it were not.

But Ruth became upset with each generalized attack and more frustrated that she could not defend the honor of the people who were now her people. She could not think of them as lizards and yet she knew the townspeople were right. These Visitors were destroying the Earth.

At night she would argue. She spoke to Hadad. But her argument was with herself. He listened. There was nothing to say.

Occasionally she would go down during the day to talk to Madge. At first she did not identify her whereabouts. Madge knew, as Jerry did, that she was camped in the forest above the house with Hadad, with Dave, as they called him. But the older ones had not known and she did not say anything that would include them in her secret.

Tony was not so cautious. He had come in from school as she had sat at the kitchen table drinking tea.

"Why are you living in the woods with that lizard?" he asked turning up his nose, as had become the local custom when the lizards were mentioned.

"Why do you call him that, Tony?"

"That's what Mrs. Hardesty calls him." He had answered with the taunt of his nine-year-old assumed authority.

Madge had apologized, sent the boy out to play, and tried to change the subject. But Mrs. Hardesty had caught the message and had begun to badger Ruth.

"No decent folks would have to do with the likes of him."

"But you don't know him, Mrs. Hardesty." Ruth had tried to defend him.

"I know everything I need to know."

Ruth had told him of the encounter when he came back that night. She had cried, frustrated that she could not defend him, could not defend herself. She was trapped by the truth.

Hadad had held her while she cried herself to sleep and then he had gone to sit in the old cave, to watch the night descend on Vida.

He had been wrong to let her stay. He had been wrong to let her know who he was. He had been wrong to let her eyes draw him to her, draw him off his guard, draw him into the world of Earth ones with their fears and angers. He did not return to the tent that night, but curled into the spot he had hollowed to fit him exactly and faced out into the night, sleeping peacefully as he had before Ruth had come back to change his life, his thoughts, his patterns.

The hover craft came closer and closer to Vida, according to each day's report. As he had promised, Jerry began to make preparations to move his entire family. He found a car for sale that could keep up with his truck and bought it with what little money he had stashed away. Daily he provisioned the truck, re-packed and reoutfitted it. He checked the engine for every possible problem, and when he had finished with the truck, he started working over the car, packing and repacking the trunk, checking and re-checking the engine. Hadad watched him from the hillside.

Hadad did not return to the upper clearing. He bought other things in town to replace the provisions that he had left with Ruth. He needed clean clothes and so he bought them, new blankets and so he replaced the ones he had had. At first she had begged him to come back to the tent. He had explained as carefully as he could that it was wrong.

She had argued, suggesting his responsibility for her, for the child. She had cried.

He could not bring himself to return because he saw only her unhappiness and frustration. He stayed away, hoping she would go away and forget the pain she was experiencing with him. He stayed away, and he longed to go back.

He returned late from his search for food. Twilight had already filled the gorge. In a few moments it would be night, suddenly, without the gradual fade of day. He circled his cave as usual and was again surprised to find Ruth sitting on the blankets. There was a wooden bowl before her full of sprouts and seeds. She took a few to nibble, lost in thought, not hearing him as he came into the clearing. She looked up as he approached.

"I needed to talk."

He sat beside her. She wandered from thought to thought, more breaking the silence than conveying ideas. As she talked she reached for handfuls of the food before her and munched them nonchalantly. Automatically, without conscious thought, Hadad imitated her actions and put the food into his mouth. The conversation was pleasant to him, needed to ease the longing.

But he did not speak, and after the casual conversation was exhausted, Ruth looked at him with sadness in her eyes. Tears rose behind her eyes. And then he did not know what to say.

"Why won't you come back?"

"I cannot be with you."

"You were with me."

"No, Ruth. It cannot be."

The tears came, and behind them the frustrations. All her unspoken disappointments, all her unfulfilled desires—all came pouring from her with accusations that he had not tried to make it work. Hadad sat in confusion, listening to all the things about him that had annoyed her, things that were a part of him that he could not change, that were the rhythm of his life, that defined him as a lizard, gave him integrity as a being not of this planet. And every argument she poured out confirmed his knowing that he could not be with her. And with each new awareness of differences even he had not seen before, new pain wrenched at his inner feelings, taking her further and further from him, leaving him more and more alone.

"You look at me with that cold stare," she sobbed. "You never let me see any of your feelings at all. I can't stand it, Hadad." The sobs choked her words. "You're so far away."

He wanted to reach to her from the distance he now felt. But he could approach only with truth. And he knew the truth would make it worse.

"Please say *something*."

"What do you want from me?"

"I want to see what you feel."

"For that you must see my own eyes."

"Then let me see them."

"Ruth, I am not a human. My eyes are not like yours."

She cried harder.

He knew he should not, but the desire to reach her

with truth, to have her acceptance as he was, became stronger in him. And so he took the lenses from his eyes and looked back at her, for the first time able to see her without the limits of those tiny holes. She was magnificent in full range. He had not risked looking at her before with his full sight. Now he was overwhelmed with desire. Her strength, the set of her jaw, her sharply contoured neck and shoulders, all looked less alien. Except for the surface, she could have been from his home. Now, seeing her in full familiarity, he could not stay away, he knew he must go back and try to make peace with the differences that disturbed her so.

And then he looked at her eyes. She was watching him, trying in the fading light to see his eyes, to see into his eyes. But she could not. The differences disturbed her and her face contorted with repugnance and she tried again to hold back tears.

He wanted to comfort her. Perhaps his voice would be enough of the familiar to soften the intensity she was experiencing. He tried to speak. But as he opened his mouth, he became suddenly aware of the mistake he had made earlier. He had eaten the grasses and seeds. And now they had their natural effect upon his body.

He had only just returned from his evening feeding, not yet digested fully the fur from the rodents, the carapaces from the insects, the feathers from the robin. And the grasses had stopped the digestion and clenched the muscles of his torso in automatic contractions designed to remove the undigested food as rapidly as possible. He had not time to move away into the forest. Immediately he regurgitated the mice, the crickets, the bird, the swift. His eyes closed automatically as the muscles continued their rhythmic surging.

From beside him he heard the choked screams. They were bleats, deep and grating. And then came the acrid smell and the coughs and then tears, and then sobs, and then small shrieks, and then the crackle of leaves and branches as the cries moved farther and farther away down the mountain.

Chapter 8

"Who ordered reconnaissance ships into the mountains?" Paul barked at Eleanor as he entered her quarters.

"You know I did," she answered with the smug assurance that was more familiar in Diana than in the pliant science officer.

"I can't see how that serves your scientific venture, Eleanor. And so I am led to believe it was not your idea, but Jeffrey's. And Jeffrey is not running the military maneuvers of this ship, is that clear?"

"Actually what is not clear is whether or not you are running the military maneuvers of this ship, Paul. We have established a clear base in Prineville. Even the resistance there has been almost eliminated. We have accomplished our first objective. Either we extend our operations from here, or we appear exceedingly complacent, my dear."

"The operations in Bend, Redmond, and Madras need personnel. Since we are all limited to three hours on the surface, and then must wait the interminable seventy-two hours before returning, we lack mobility, Eleanor. And until you perfect that antitoxin, we can't afford the privilege of personal endeavor. There is no advantage in moving up into the mountain gorge."

"No advantage to you, perhaps. But there are other purposes to be served."

"Not scientific ones."

She paused, raised an eyebrow, and took a more subtle tone of voice. "No, not scientific ones. I'd even go so far as to say military ones, if that weren't risking insulting your perspicacity."

"Whose military purposes?"

"There is a potential saboteur out there, Paul. Jeffrey has found out where he is. He is going to find him and carry out Diana's orders. That hardly seems inappropriate. What seems suspect is why you did not order the mission yourself when Jeffrey told you where Hadad was hiding. Apparently it serves you to keep the priest alive. But then that might suggest sympathy with the fifth column, and one would not think to accuse a military commander of . . . what is it the Earthlings say? 'Speaking with forked tongue!' Just who do you serve, Paul?"

"I serve The Leader, Eleanor, not the whims of Diana, nor of Jeffrey. There is no purpose in this personal vendetta. You have been persuaded to pursue a fruitless endeavor, and to violate the boundaries of your own authority." He paused to assess her reaction, looking for a gap in her convictions. He found none. And so he stepped to the door, opened it, and ordered the guards he had stationed there to confine her to her quarters.

He glanced back as she went to the console to reach beyond his authority for help.

"That won't work, Eleanor. I've already given orders that your requests are to be ignored and all communications are to go through my hands directly. You've chosen your allies poorly, my dear."

He smiled and left, pleased to see the anger aroused in his victim, content now that his opponent had been suppressed.

Chapter 9

Hadad sat for a moment looking down at the lenses in his hand. The muscles in his abdomen pulsed. Ruth's cries as she descended the mountain did not stop. Eventually he could not hear them anymore, but they continued inside him. And only when he could allow them to subside did the convulsions stop.

He reached into a pocket for the liquid he always carried. He would have to clean the lenses before he returned them to his eyes again. He stood and kicked dirt over the decaying mass in front of him. He would return later and add the leaves to freshen the area. For now, he could think only of the need for his lenses.

He went back to the campsite in the old trees and boiled water on Ruth's stove. He looked at the tent, at her things, at his clothes still on the string under the tarp she had strung as a shelter from the rain. This could never be again. He knew that now, and then decided to take the clean clothes, bury the ones he was wearing that smelled of the vomited meat that had touched them.

The water boiled, and he cleaned the lenses and returned them to his eyes. He placed them carefully, and the world returned to the peephole reality that he had accustomed himself to for months. He put drops in his eyes to ease the rubbing on his lids.

Methodically he replaced things in the camp and then returned to the cave and cleaned the entrance, found rue and sage and mint and rubbed them to spread them over the tainted ground.

He heard the hover craft. He knew then that it must be high above him because it could not have navigated the gorge without lights, and he could see none. They were coming up the canyon. He had to warn Jerry, make sure he got the family out of Vida before morning. It was cloudy, no moon. They had to leave soon.

The path down the mountain was well worn. As he reached the garden he could still hear the hover craft above him. It had turned and was heading east. He crossed to the house and pounded on the door.

He waited only a moment and then pounded again. And then there was shuffling behind the door and Jerry's voice muffled by the heavy wood.

"Who is it?"

"It's Dave. They're overhead. You have to go."

"It's *him*." Mrs. Hardesty's voice came from behind the door.

"Get me my rifle, Madge." Jerry's voice.

More shuffling.

"Jerry, open the door. You've got to listen to me."

The door opened and a rifle edged through the crack. Hadad did not wait for an explanation, he jumped to the side of the porch and, hugging the building, ducking the windows, he ran back toward the forest. In the moment the door had opened he had seen Ruth, back by the far wall. She had told them. There was no other explanation.

Shots rang across the garden, and then footsteps followed. Only one person followed. The steps were heavy, probably Jerry's. Hadad could easily outrun him. He climbed the path, and when he reached the first ridge he cut west around the mountain, leaving the path, risking the additional noise as he cut through the underbrush, listening for sounds to tell him how far he had out distanced his pursuer.

He had gained a few yards, but Jerry was following

him easily. He cut up the mountain, through the old trees, back down to the east, staying high until he had gained more space between them. And then he climbed into the densest of the old trees. They were noble pines, hard to climb, with no branches low to anchor a hand or foot for leverage. He shinned up the rough bark and his clothing tore as he moved.

Once in the shelter of the branches, he sat incredibly still. He listened to his pulse slowing deliberately. He watched, and listened for the sounds of man in the forest below. Jerry came to the tree he had climbed, passed it, came back, sat beneath him, swore at the ground, looked into the darkness all around him, leaned back into the tree, and then got up and returned down the mountain.

Hadad could not stay in that spot. He waited for a while and then carefully dropped to the ground. He would have to leave. He needed his jacket from the cave. He carefully worked his way back to the clearing, circled to make sure no one waited there for him. The clearing was empty. He found the jacket, took the things he needed, put them into his pocket, and started east to the road. He would cut down beyond Jerry's farm, walk the forest parallel to the road until he passed the town, then try to catch a ride west.

He crossed Angel's Flight Road and slipped into the trees on the other side. Carefully he edged down to the highway and behind the houses that staked claim to the level ground beside it, lighted markers in the moonless, starless night.

He heard footsteps on the covered bridge and voices. And then as he slipped behind the Cooper barn, he heard a shout: "There he is," and a shot followed him into the forest. Again he climbed into the forest. But now there were too many following to listen for his pursuers. They spread in a fan behind him. He could not maneuver around them; all he had to his advantage was speed.

He headed west, but the forest grew thicker there. It reached sharp fingers at him, tore at the clothes that were already shredded, ripped at the plastic beneath the thin covering. Blackberry bushes threaded between the trees in a thicket, and he had to rip himself out of their clutches. A briar caught his pants, and as he pulled one leg free, the other was grabbed by several more thorns. Voices came around the thicket. He pulled out of the pants and cut back to the east. He could run more freely through the aspens, but the voices gained on him and so he climbed into the underbrush again. Miscalculating the branches, he was caught here and there and tore free, gradually ripping the plastic from his body, exposing more and more of the mottled green and black beneath. He brushed aside a bush, caught his hand and ripped it, pushed through yet another bush, and found himself back at Angel's Flight Road. He would have to cross, try to get to the other side without cover. He dove across the road, and just as he reached the shadows of the other side, he heard a woman's scream right in front of him.

He pulled away to his right and dove for the forest. But a hissed whisper stopped him.

"No. Come here."

He looked back in the direction of the voice. It was Ruth, standing by the open trunk of her car.

"Come here," she whispered urgently.

He edged back to the car, watching for pursuers on the road and in the forest on the other side. There was no one yet.

"Get in the trunk," she whispered.

He looked at her for a moment, and then obeyed.

As she closed the trunk on him, he saw the men on the road beyond her. They were running toward the car. And then there was blackness. He froze, trying to

still his breathing. He had either found refuge or
stepped into his own death. He was not sure.

Boots pounded on the pavement toward the car.

"Are you all right?" It was Jerry's voice.

"Oh, Jerry, he looked so awful." Ruth sobbed the
words. There had been no tears before the words.

"He was here?"

"He came out of the forest over there. I was afraid
he was going to come at me, but he didn't. He ran
down the road, toward the highway, then up into the
forest, over there."

"Come on, men. We'll get that lizard." Another
voice.

Then Jerry's.

"Ruth, are you going to be all right?"

"Oh, Jerry. It was so awful. I never realized . . ."
She sobbed again.

"We were both fooled. Don't blame yourself. Why
don't you go back to the house to Madge? You'll be all
right there."

"I can't stay here, Jerry. I don't want to know. I
don't want to know you've killed him. But I don't
want to think he's still out there." She cried now, tears
that seemed as real as the ones she had cried earlier
running down the mountain.

"Go on back to the house."

"I want to get out of here."

"You shouldn't try to drive. You're too upset."

"Let me go, Jerry. Just let me get out of here."

"Will you be careful?"

"I've got to go."

"Okay. Okay. Have you got everything you need?"

"It's all in the car. The trunk is full."

"Drive carefully, Ruth."

"I will. Be careful yourself."

"We'll be all right."

"Yeah."

Boots moved away down the road. Hadad expected the trunk to open. It did not. There were lighter steps, then the door opening, closing. And then the ignition. He braced for the turns as the car moved into the road. The brakes squealed. He was thrown back as the car gunned forward, and then tossed from side to side as the car took the turns. She had gone west. He was not certain of life. All he knew was that death was not immediate, and so he slept.

He woke when the car stopped. The ignition was not turned off; other cars were idling beside him. Gradually the trunk space filled with exhaust. He took the knife from the jacket pocket and pressed on the valve of the spare tire and took a deep breath of the clean air that escaped. In a few moments the engines were turned off. He rationed his clean air, struggling as long as he could with the fumes around him. He was not certain where he was or how long he would be there.

The door opened.

"No, I can't open the trunk, officer. I haven't got the key with me. My brother has it in town."

"Then we'll just have to shoot the lock, lady. Nobody goes through without a thorough inspection. That's the orders."

"You will not shoot that lock."

"Won't hurt nothin' inside."

"Unless it does."

"Not likely."

"But how about the lock?"

"That's the breaks, lady."

"You shoot that lock, and I'm sunk. I can't afford to replace it, and everything I own is in that trunk. Forget it."

"Then you forget coming on this road, or any other road. We're not taking any chances. You see those tanks? They're ready to stop any invasion of the valley right here. We've got these on the roads, and antiair-craft on the mountains. There's going to be one place on Earth for human beings even if they take the rest of the planet."

"But I *am* a human being."

"No chances, lady. That's orders. I shoot that lock, or you turn back. That's all there is."

"Then I turn back."

"Your choice. You can use the shoulder there."

The steps moved away from the car, the door opened and closed, and the engine started again. Hadad was thrown hard against the back as the car edged out onto the shoulder and across the median into the eastbound lane.

The car continued for about twenty minutes and then it stopped again. This time the door opened and closed, there were footsteps, a key in the lock, and the trunk opened.

The moon had come up and the sudden brightness was startling. Hadad turned and tried to sit up.

"Watch your head. Here, let me help you out."

He crouched in the space and swung first one leg, then the other, out over the bumper and down to the ground. His knees were shaky from the long run and the cramped curl he had held while he slept. He stretched, leaning against the car with one hand. Ruth closed the trunk.

"You might as well ride up front with me." She looked down at his bare legs, strips of the plastic skin hanging from them, green beneath the rips. "You're going to need a medicine plant."

"Yes."

"And another pair of pants." She laughed. "You don't even look like a respectable Visitor dressed like that."

Hadad sighed, the tension of the evening lessened, not gone.

"I've got a pair of leathers in the backseat. They'll probably fit you. After all, I made them for *you*."

She moved to the side of the car, opened the back door, and got out a pair of pants like the legs of a deer. They were larger than the ones Hadad had seen at the store, cut to fit the larger muscles in his legs, cut like the pants that had been hanging on the line. He put them on. They were soft. They fit perfectly. He looked up at her, uncertain of what to say.

"We better get on the way; go on, get in." Ruth spoke first.

"Thank you."

"Go on, get in."

Hadad got into the passenger seat. He waited while Ruth rummaged in the backseat, then shut the back door and got in behind the wheel. She handed him a canvas bag.

"There are bandages and needles, thread, pins, in there. You better get yourself patched up. I don't know who we're going to run into, but you look like hell. There may be something else back there that will fit you. Better get rid of the jacket too. We may have to go back through Vida."

"To Vida?"

"I'm not certain. We can't get through the road-block. They're doing full body searches back there. Nearly ripped my cheek off trying to make sure I wasn't a lizard."

"Ruth, you must go alone. It is not use for me to try to run farther."

"You mean useful."

"Oh, yes, useful. It is not useful for me to try to run farther."

"It's my fault they were chasing you out of Vida. I shouldn't have said anything to Jerry, but I thought he would understand. Really I did. He came up into the woods when he heard me crying. I was so tired of lying. I had to tell someone the truth."

"You don't have to explain."

"Maybe I do. Maybe I have to explain to me. I betrayed you. And I didn't mean to." Her voice broke, but there were no tears to follow.

"I am sorry I have brought you so much trouble. I am sorry to be in your life. I am a lizard. I am sorry I cannot be a human for you." Hadad looked down at the canvas bag.

"That's hubris."

"What?"

"Hubris—pride. One can apologize for what one does. But when one apologizes for being human, that is playing God—hubris. The Greeks considered that the tragic flaw in man. I guess for you to apologize for being lizard is the same thing. You are what you are."

"And you, you are what you are?"

"That I'm not so certain about. Sometimes it's easier to accept your lizardness than it is to face my humanness. I should have kept my mouth shut when Jerry asked why I was crying. I should have lied, anything but tell him the truth."

" 'Should have'? That sounds like something we both ate for dinner." He watched her as slowly the realization came to her of what had happened to both of their dinners, as slowly she realized he had made light of the catastrophe that had precipitated the betrayal she regretted, the mad dash through the forest, the terrifying drive down the mountain. Slowly a grin started in her eyes and spread across her face. And then he laughed himself.

Chapter 10

"There. There's the covered bridge. That's where they said he'd be . . . Captain, we've found the town. Do we burn them out?" The pilot's voice crackled over the radio.

"No, I'm going to try to land. I want to see that lizard squirm. Go on down the canyon," Jeffrey's voice replied.

Paul monitored from his own craft. Patricia rode beside him. They were alone. They traveled without lights, making no radio contact, paralleling the search party, but in the crevice to the north beyond the mountains that rimmed the river gorge.

"Fool. He's caught up in his own vendetta. He must be eliminated. Patricia."

"Yes, sir."

Paul smiled. He enjoyed the formality Patricia insisted upon. He could count on it always, even in his bed. There was never a moment when she presumed. He liked that. And he could trust it. She was a good fighter pilot as well. Useful!

He turned his attention back to the radio transmissions.

"I can't land. We'll have to smoke him out."

"Shall I turn back, Captain?"

"No, we're on top of this. Let us know what's up ahead."

"Shall I intercept, Commander?" Patricia broke his reverie.

"No," Paul sighed. "Keep out of sight."

Chapter 11

There was a low rumble in the air above them as the hover craft scouted the gorge, this time penetrating between the canyon walls.

"Turn off your lights, and drive very fast."

Ruth snapped off the lights just as the craft passed over the car. She accelerated quickly and the volley of shots hit the road behind them.

"They mean business. Damn, I wish I could see. I have to find a gravel road off to the left. I know it's here somewhere; we're almost back to Vida."

"You can slow down. They are continuing down the canyon. They aren't after us. Not this time."

The tires squealed as she took the turn she hadn't expected. The covered bridge of Vida appeared suddenly in front of them.

"I missed it. I've got to get turned around. Get down. I don't want anyone here to see you in the car."

Hadad crouched beneath the dashboard and Ruth pulled into a driveway and backed into the highway, turning west again. The lights were still out and so she traveled slowly around the curves, hunting for the road that would take them over the crest into the next valley.

Cannon fire shook the air and lighted the sky, outlining the ridges around them. The hover craft returned fire and the brighter pulses of light gave them seconds of illumination. In the third round Ruth spotted the elusive road. It was hardly more than a driveway, but it opened up above the main road and curved gradually up through the forest. They were well off the highway by the time the rest of the hover craft dove through the valley, firing at random as they came.

Hadad looked back to see the old wooden bridge at Goodpasture Road break into flames. He wished that Jerry and his family had left, but he knew Jerry was too upset to give up the chase. A third craft strafed the village as it came, and Hadad watched the flames and knew the farm had been hit. The first flash would have set fire to the house. And the second would have hit the truck and the extra gas cans Jerry had filled the day before. A fireball erupted and sparks caught the scrapwood, drifted up into the higher branches of the surrounding trees.

Flames leaped into the trees surrounding the river, scorched the banks, then climbed the mountains on each side of the gorge. Brightened, the contours of the canyon were easy to identify; illuminated from below, the hover craft became readily visible as huge white dragons spitting fire onto the ground.

Balls of fire blew into the sky as each house was consumed in the fire storm. Small explosions delineated the passage of the blaze as it found stored gas cans, waiting cars and trucks, the gas station in Leaburg to the west.

Hadad glanced into the backseat of the car. The tent was not there.

"You have not your camp things."

"I was just loading when you crossed the road. I had to leave them."

"They will be gone with the fire."

"I know. Madge and Jerry . . ."

"Yes."

"If only they'd gone."

"Ruth, sometimes there is no place to go."

"What do you mean?"

"Jerry had no place to go. He just did not care to

fight. At least not the war. I have no place to go either."

"I'm headed up to . . . a friend's. We can stay there. It's possible the Visitors will pass us by. His place is way up in the mountains."

"Ruth, I am prepared to die."

"Well, I'm not."

They drove on in silence. They traveled without lights, but the sky was lighted with the flash of the fighting, and the forest fire illuminated the crest behind them. It was slow, climbing, turning, scraping past bushes, dodging the larger rocks that had fallen into the road. As they topped the ridge, another hover craft appeared, this one cruising without lights down the next canyon.

"Stop the car. Let them pass," Hadad ordered.

Ruth braked to a stop. The white phantom crossed about three hundred yards in front of them.

"They had to have seen us."

"Not necessarily."

"Hadad, we're the only thing moving on the mountain."

"The brush is thick. Without lights the car is not so obvious as you think. They did not see us or they would have opened fire."

"What do we do now?"

"Wait to see if they turn back. If not, then we go on."

The craft turned and came back up the ridge.

"Do not move, Ruth. They may pass again."

Slowly the craft glided over the car, this time directly overhead.

"Hadad, I . . ."

"Shhh."

The craft passed and continued east. For several minutes they sat, listening.

"You can drive now."

"They might . . ."

"It is all right, Ruth. The craft is gone."

Ruth started the car again and continued the slow, painstaking trail across the ridge and down into the canyon on toward Wendling. She was frightened, but the hazards of the narrow road navigated without lights soon occupied her attention.

At Wendling the road was paved. At Marcola they turned north. Hours later they reached the highway at Sweet Home.

"I need gas." Ruth headed west on the highway, searching for a station that still had fuel. Most had during the winter. But the invasion of Prineville had disrupted the order of things as the state prepared itself for war. She passed one station with large signs—NO GAS—and continued on. There was traffic on the highway, and a chain of brake lights wove back toward them.

"Another roadblock, damn." Ruth waited for a clearing in the traffic and spun the car into a U turn and headed back up the highway away from the block.

There was a small station in Cascadia with no signs. She pulled in and they looked for an attendant. No one was around. She got out and tried the pump, not expecting it to work. It did. She had put in about half a tank when an old man in coveralls came around the corner of the station.

"Hey, lady, you can't pump that. It's against the law. You should know better; you've got Oregon plates. That's the law."

"I'm glad you're here. I need it filled."

"Can't do it. We're rationing."

"I have to get to Detroit."

"Can't get to twenty-two. The army's got the summit. Best you can do is go on down to Albany. Maybe you can get gas there."

"How do you stay here, with the Visitors so close?"

"I pray, lady."

The old man pumped another five gallons into her tank, and charged her double what the pump said. Ruth didn't argue. She got back into the car, and Hadad watched the old man stash the bills in his pocket and head back around the corner of the station. As they pulled out onto the highway, Hadad noticed a station wagon in the back and the old man getting in the tail, probably going back to his nap until the next customer tried to pump some gas.

Ruth headed west again.

"You can leave me and go to Albany, the way he said."

"I don't know if we'll make it, but I think I'd rather try the back road across the mountain. I've driven it before. It isn't too bad."

"Ruth . . . I don't know . . ."

"I don't either. I don't know where we're going. I don't have any idea what I'm even going to do when we get there. All I know is—" She started to cry and then stopped. "I don't know anymore why I'm with you. At least before I could say I wanted to be with you. That made it all okay somehow. It didn't matter, or maybe it did, that nobody accepted. I don't know what I feel. I'm not certain I feel anything. It's all numb inside."

She found the road that ran up between the reservoirs and turned automatically. She went on talking and the words started to run together with gaps in the history where Hadad could fill in his own impressions, his own memories.

He listened. He could not help her. The values she struggled with were not his values. He listened as she described her search for someplace to settle, to work, to love, to put down the love she wanted so much to give; the fear that there would not be a world for her child to grow up in, that there would not be a world for her to grow up in. She was frightened and missed the stillness around her as the car climbed past the reservoir and up another grade.

The battle was well behind them. No craft slid overhead, no cannon fired into the air above them. The night was still, and crickets, unaware of the seriousness of the issues at hand, chirped their messages to one another across the mountain meadows.

Chapter 12

The sound of the forest fire crackled through the radio and the voices of the hover-craft pilots shouted above the excitement. Paul listened.

"That's it, Captain. We got them all. Nobody even ran."

"There's a lot of smoke; pull up so you don't get caught in it. Pull up, I say."

"Captain, there are people running down the road."

"Open fire."

Paul shrugged. "Waste of good meat."

"Pardon me, Commander?"

"Nothing, Patricia. Just an observation."

"Yes, sir."

The shots popped through the radio in a rough staccato.

"Captain, we're in trouble. Cannons . . ."

The more distant transmission came from the scout ship down canyon. There was no response from the marauding pack over Vida. There was the sound of cannon fire and then the explosion and then the radio transmission went dead. It was unmistakably the end of the scout ship. Paul waited for some response from the other ships, for an order to turn back and avoid the confrontation, some warning about what lay ahead in the canyon, some strategy, but there was none.

"Damn fools turned off their radios and missed the warning. They're headed right into the ambush."

"Shall I try to intercept them, Commander?"

"No, Patricia. They were foolish enough to embark

on this endeavor. Let them find their own solutions. Vida is gone. And the decision as to what to do about the priest is moot. You heard them, no one escaped the fire storm. I'd say Jeffrey got his way this time."

"Yes, Commander."

The radios crackled back onto the air as the pilots worked out their strategies, navigating the narrow gorge, keeping low by the river that wound down the western slope of the Cascades. They flew directly into the path of the antiaircraft guns and one by one they came under heavy fire. There were shouts to pull up, to turn back, to return fire, and the interchange of shots lighted the sky in the next canyon and etched the silhouette of the range before them against a red-orange night sky. Fire began to edge over the mountains, licking up the forests, dryer than usual because of the disruption of the evaporation cycle by the removal of water from the major reservoirs for the mother ship storage tanks.

So much water had been pumped and then returned to Earth by the intervention of the resistance forces. But not every mother ship had been attacked, and enough water had been taken from the planet to shift the rainy seasons in much of the country. Oregon was particularly affected, and the now-dry timber crackled in the dry air. Rain clouds had gathered. But the rain had not fallen. And so the fire blazed on, eating up the acres and acres of wood, cresting the ridge now and working down into the next canyon.

"Commander, over there. There was movement, just a minute ago. I don't see anything now, but I could swear something moved over the crest down there in the trees. This side of the fire, sir. There. Down there."

"I don't see anything. Double back. Let me have another look."

"Yes, sir."

The craft turned and came back up the canyon. Paul scouted the area, searching between the dark trees that had not yet burned. He saw nothing.

"Keep going, Patricia. If something did move, it is more likely to continue on its way if it thinks we didn't spot it. There are deer in the forests below. You may have seen them fleeing the fire."

"It looked more like an automobile or a truck, sir."

"Keep going; I'm watching."

Paul watched the forest as they passed overhead. There was a large shadowy mass on the stones beneath the craft, but it was hard to distinguish a pattern because of the trees. If it were a car, it would have come up from Vida. The hover-craft crews had not spotted a car leaving. He questioned the possibility that anyone had had time to escape the attack, but he watched the patterns of light and dark on the planet below them.

"Continue on, beyond that ridge, then double back. But climb a little higher and reduce your speed after you turn. Maybe if we don't stir up the air so much, your animal down there will move again, figure he can escape."

"Yes, Commander."

The craft maneuvered through the canyon, turned, and began a slower run. Below them the shadow escaped the trees and continued down the ribbon path of whitish stones.

"Sharp eyes, Patricia. That is a car. Now the question is, who's inside?"

"Shall I open fire, Commander?"

"No, Patricia, just follow, preferably just above them, and out of sight; use the cloud cover. Let's see where they go."

The craft made figure eights to slow its forward progress to that of the automobile below. When the road became more visible beneath them and the inevitable path more obvious, they circled back over the terrain to give the driver more space to maneuver without seeing them. Paul did not want to risk detection. If the driver felt he was getting away from the Visitor attack, escaping the disaster, that was better. It would not pay to keep the watch too tight and be spotted above them, withholding fire.

The car turned north at the intersection, heading farther up into the mountains. The craft followed, waiting for some indication of the contents of the car, some sign of who had escaped Vida.

Chapter 13

Cloud cover obscured the starlight.

"Hadad, I have to turn on the lights. I can't see the road."

"I know. Turn them on."

Hadad searched the sky and the horizon. They had left the Mackenzie River gorge far behind them. Another range separated them from the raging forest fire. They could still smell the smoke, but ashes no longer fell on the road as they drove. Again the isolation of the mountains surrounded them with the illusion that all was at peace.

The road wound up the mountain, maintained here as a one-lane road, there as a two-lane road, another place as a gravel path. There were markers with numbers, numbers that related to some system, some order, some pattern that someone understood or had understood when the road was built.

The headlights caught a deer on the edge of the road as they came around one corner. Ruth stopped and the deer watched them and then turned into the forest. Bright spots reflected the lights on either side of the road as they drove, and Hadad found he was identifying the animals by their height and the distance between their eyes. He wondered if his assumptions were correct.

When they reached the ridge near Minniece Point, Hadad heard the hover craft.

"Turn out the lights," he demanded, and Ruth did so immediately, also braking to slow the speed to the distance she could almost see in front of them.

"What is it?"

"Above us. Listen."

The craft droned, hardly louder than the tree frogs they had heard earlier, but deeper in pitch.

"It's directly overhead."

Ruth stopped the car and leaned out the window to look up.

"I don't see anything but clouds."

"They have been following us."

"But why?"

"Ruth, I am hunted by my people. Leave me here on the mountain. Go on without me. Go back to the roadblocks and join the resistance to save your planet. You cannot help me now."

"Hadad, I won't leave you here."

"You are being foolish."

"Maybe."

It was easier to see the road now that their eyes had adjusted to the darkness. Ruth started the car and edged forward, watching the growth beside the road to find turns. She drove slowly. They both listened for a change in the drone above them.

"Why don't they open fire on us? They must know we are here."

"They know."

"Then why don't they get it over with?"

"I don't know."

The road began to descend into the valley beyond. Once again they found patches of pavement with white lines that glowed in the minimal light, edging the one-lane road.

And then there was a thunderous crack above their heads, and a flash of intense blue light that illuminated everything for an instant and then disappeared, leaving everything darker than before. Ruth screamed and jammed her foot onto the brake, throwing them both against the dashboard, hitting her head against the rim of the steering wheel. Hadad felt the rigidity in all of his muscles, the impulse to freeze compounded by the movement of his body in the car. He was certain the ship above them had opened fire and missed. But the sound was directly above them, and he knew the ship's weaponry was too accurate to come that close without doing damage.

He looked out into the darkness. They were alive. He was not certain how or why, but they were alive.

And then it began to rain.

Ruth leaned against the steering wheel, her head against the rim. Hadad worried that she was unconscious and moved across the seat to examine her injuries. She was not bleeding and was not unconscious, but her breathing was shallow. As he pulled her back from the wheel, she started to cry. He did not stop her. Now he held her, cradling her head between his cheek and shoulder, holding her torso with his strong arms, letting her sobs release the tension. He wished he, too, could cry.

The drone above them was gone.

There was only the persistent hammering of rain powering down on the roof and hood of the car.

It is likely that for a moment they both fell asleep. Hadad could not remember feeling his shoulder beginning to tingle where her head rested, but now he felt the numbness. The rain was still beating on the metal of the car, steady and strong.

"Ruth . . . Ruth, wake up."

"Hmmm?"

"Wake up. We have to get off the mountain."

"What?"

"It was only lightning. We are alive."

"What happened?"

"I don't know. The hover craft is gone. We can turn the lights on. We are tired. Let's go."

"Let me sleep."

"Ruth, the water is deep in the road now, and moving fast. The road may flood. We would be washed down the mountain. We have to try to get to your friend."

Ruth wailed a reply, trying to return to sleep.

"Ruth, listen to me. We must get off the mountain."

Hadad reached across her and opened the window, then he pushed her body toward the door and thrust her head out into the cooling rain. She woke instantly, struggling to pull away from the water, away from his grasp.

"What are you doing to me?"

"Good, you are awake. Now you can drive us away from here."

Ruth started the car, turned on the windshield wipers and the lights, and started through the storm. She did not seem to remember her resistance to waking, and Hadad did not remind her.

They had driven slowly before without lights. Now they drove more slowly with them. Water puddled on the road, ran gushing over the side and down the embankments, fell in torrents from the clouds above, from the overhanging cliffs above, dripping from the trees around them. Carefully they picked their way.

The road branched in front of them and Ruth became confused. The left fork seemed more traveled and so Hadad suggested they turn that way. Ruth did not resist.

The night was too long. The air became chilled suddenly and Hadad and Ruth both reached immediately to close the windows that had been left slightly open to reduce the steaming of the windshield.

"It will be dawn soon."

"How can you tell?"

"The chill. It comes just before dawn on your planet."

The road began to descend quickly and the path

they traveled was now a raging river as well. The brakes were of little help and so Ruth put the car into the lowest forward gear the automatic transmission offered. They did not talk. And though he did not know how to operate an automobile with his body, Hadad thought the car's maneuvers, concentrating on the turns of the road, as intensely as Ruth.

They crossed a bridge and a few hundred yards later saw the first sign they had been able to recognize. One arrow pointed ahead of them DETROIT 12, the other back the way they had come, HIGHWAY 22 13. Again they crossed a bridge and then to the left they could see, even in the dark rain, the open expanse of a lake.

The road twisted between the lake and the steep hill to the right, down, closer and closer to the water. Trees guarded the lakeside, and dirt roads and driveways led to campgrounds and boat ramps.

The road became more level and Ruth relaxed more as she drove. The rain slowed and seemed almost to stop, and then suddenly there was a flash of lightning over the lake, and the sky was laced with tiny white lines for just an instant and then dark again. The thunder cracked the sky and echoed from the hills across the lake. They reached a stretch along the lake where the road, though just as wide itself, crossed a narrow stretch between the water and the hillside. Lightning struck and illuminated the road ahead and gave them warning. For there, jackknifed across the narrow pavement, was a logging truck, laced together with long newly stripped trees, and then piled high with boxes and bundles tied with tarpaulins binding them to the log framework improvising the bed of a truck.

The truck had struck the pole supporting power lines that led down to the campground. Now the wires lay on the roof of the cab, and its occupants leaned out the window waving frantically, shaking their heads, yelling sounds unintelligible in the fury of the storm.

Ruth stopped the car comfortably behind the jackknifed truck and they got out to investigate. Now they could hear the shouts.

"Don't touch the truck."

Hadad recognized the danger and held Ruth back from the side of the vehicle.

"Do not touch it. You would ground the current."

"But they're okay in the truck."

"They are not grounded. You are. We must lift the cable from the truck."

"How?"

Hadad began to search the forest beside the cab.

The man in the truck shouted advice. His wife and two sons huddled on the seat beside him.

"You folks, you'd best turn back. We're stuck here. We can't get out."

Hadad heard the panic in his voice.

"You are safe in the cab. You must do as I say. Do not try to leave the cab. We will find a way to remove the wires. But you must stay there. Do you understand?"

"Yes." The man quieted, more in response to the authority in Hadad's voice than in response to the words.

Hadad found the tree he was looking for and went back to where Ruth was standing.

"We need tools."

"Most of them are still . . ."

"We need an ax."

"I have a small one in my backpack."

"It will have to do."

Hadad took the short-handled hatchet that Ruth dug from the backpack and examined its edge. The blade was sharp. What it lacked in size it compensated for in quality. It was not an ax, but it would do.

He returned to the forest near the front of the cab and scaled up the tree he had chosen for the task. When he reached the level of the roof of the cab he began stripping the branches, revealing a fork in the limb that could hold the wires as had the pole nearby.

When he had prepared the tree sufficiently he climbed down, clinging to the side of the tree below the branches. When he reached the ground he looked up at the people in the cab to be sure they were not trying to get out. He saw the same look as he had seen on the Earth ones when he did the pushups. And then he realized that he had climbed as a lizard, not as a man would climb. He looked away from the dumb-struck faces. He did not have time for their confusion now.

Ruth had been watching from the road, her hair now soaked, plastered to her face. He pulled her back to the car.

"I'm all right. I don't mind being wet."

"Get in. I need your help."

They each got into the front seat and Hadad paused, considering alternatives.

"I need a large hook of some kind. Something that will hold the wires."

"You're not going to try to lift those wires, are you? They're still live. You could . . ."

"Ruth, I need a hook, a large hook. Do you have anything that will work as a hook?"

"Hadad, all I have is my leather tools."

"Let me see them."

She kneeled and leaned over the back of the seat. From the floor behind her she pulled a leather bag. She settled back onto the seat and opened the draw-string, pulling the bag out into a large circle on which the tools lay.

The punch opened in a V shape. Nothing else even resembled a hook. Hadad took the punch and tested its rigidity. It was sprung open. It would work.

"Is that all you need?"

"No. Now I need a cord that will not conduct electricity."

"I can't help you."

"Yes, you can. The plastic that covers my body. It will not conduct electricity. It will burn. But if it is thick enough, it will not burn quickly, even if the cable sparks. The thing you call braid, you can do that?"

"Yes."

"Good."

Hadad took the leather clothes and pulled them away from his body. He took the leather-cutting knife from the array of tools and began carefully to cut the strips away from his legs and then to cut thin strips up his chest, handing the strips to Ruth as fast as he could cut them.

At first she sat confused, but gradually she began to understand what he wanted, and as he handed her strips, she worked them into a long braid fastened at one end to one handle of the leather punch. He continued to cut until she had braided a strip about three feet long. It had taken strips from his legs, from his torso, from his upper arms, from his sides and buttocks and part of his back, but the cord was made and it was strong.

He dressed again in leather, now able to feel even more intensely the roughness of the wet skins.

He took the rope from Ruth and left the car, feeling the rain again against his body, colder now in the wet leather.

A tree grew beside the tree he had shaped, this one taller, broader, with limbs leaning out over the road, almost reaching to the truck itself. This tree he climbed, this time remembering to climb as a man would climb, finding the lodgings for feet in the lower branches. He climbed out the limb toward the truck and gauged his body weight so that he did not go out so far that the limb would touch the cab.

Carefully then he lowered his flesh-colored rope down from the branch. There was a dip in the wires right behind the cab. He aimed the V-shaped hook down that crevice and pulled up, hoping to catch the wires. He missed.

He moved a little farther out on the branch. He tried again.

This time he caught the wires, but as he pulled up on the rope they slipped from the notch in the tool.

He tried again. This time he caught them and they stayed just on the lip of the punch handle. Slowly he pulled them up and over, off the cab, to the notch in the tree beside him.

A shout rose from the cab, but it was immediately drowned in thunder as lightning struck the tree that had suspended Hadad over the road, and flames licked instantly through the branches, burning the tree to its core despite the wet branches, sizzling the wet needles.

Hadad dropped to the ground, the leather shirt and pants charred and smoldering, burned through in places, revealing his mottled skin below.

The family poured from the cab and Ruth came running from the car. Hadad opened his eyes to see them ripping pieces of the burning shirt from his chest. He waited for the realization of who he was to follow, for the accusation and the terror. But there was none.

"He's burned bad. Skin's all putrid already, blisters

everywhere. Don't touch the skin. Here, help me lift him under the arm there. Boys, get his legs. You can manage. The man needs your help. Let's get him back to your car, lady."

Hadad let them carry him, aware of the need of Earth ones to respond to the needs of others, the desperation to be needed in an emergency.

They put him into the car and then the man began the arduous process of inching the truck away from the pole, straightening the truck bed on the narrow road without losing the back wheels into the soft water-soaked forest floor beside the road. Ruth sat beside him impatient with the delay, her hand beating nervously on the steering wheel.

"Do not respond rapidly. I am all right. The man needs to think I am badly burned. Otherwise he would see the truth, that my skin is not human. Do not look at me yet."

"Are you sure you're all right? The lightning."

"It went through me. I felt its power."

"And you're all right?"

"Yes, Ruth. It is power. But it is finite. It did not consume me."

"But you fell."

"No. I did not fall. I dropped to the ground to leave the fire."

"You can do that?"

"And so could you if your muscles were strong to absorb the impact."

"I don't understand."

"Believe me, and let the man worry. He needs the worry for me to give him courage to move his truck. Otherwise he would not know how to straighten it."

"How do you know that?"

"It is a very human thing, courage."

The truck veered onto the narrow shoulder and

then straightened on the narrow road. He honked and waved and then set off toward Detroit, clearing the road for Ruth to follow.

At the highway the trucker turned left; Ruth followed, but when they reached town, she turned left again and made her way down toward the school, away from the trucker and his family. When they were out of sight, she pulled to the side of the road and turned out the lights.

The sky paled with the approaching dawn; the sky was heavy with clouds and the rain continued.

"Your friend lives here in Detroit?"

Ruth nodded.

"In this house?"

"No. He's a ranger. He lives over behind the station."

She looked down at her hands twisting in her lap. "I just pulled over here to get away from the—"

"I understand."

They did not speak to break the silence. Hadad watched Ruth for a few minutes and then he looked out at the sleeping village. A single signal light flashed red in all four directions at the intersection. A sign in the café window said "open," though it clearly was not. The mountain hideaway had apparently been a refuge for vacationers, when there had been vacations, when there had been freedom of movement, freedom to choose travel, to choose departure from the ordinariness of survival. There were still a few who insisted that the world would go on unchanged, but most had given up first the pleasure of playfulness and then the desire for it.

The village itself survived. No longer a playground, now it housed the hungry, the refugees. Vegetable gardens covered expanses that probably had once been lawns, corn grew hip-high where children might have ridden bicycles and played sandlot baseball. There were no vacancies. And no recreational vehicles stood loaded with equipment to amuse the idle. Now those vehicles housed families who had escaped the lowlands, and tent villages dotted the hillsides.

"I'm hungry."

"Perhaps your friend will have food."

Ruth nodded and reached down to start the car again.

"I cannot go with you, Ruth."

She took her hand from the ignition and put it on the steering wheel, gripping it too tightly, her knuckles white.

"I seem to have traded the skin of a person for the skin of a deer. But underneath I am the same. Your friend will not accept me any more than Jerry did. I am a Visitor, Ruth."

"Where will you go?"

"Into the mountains. Eventually the red dust will put the virus in my body and I will die. Until then I will live in the mountains." He looked out at the forests around him, seeing, as he looked, the contours of land that would welcome him best, give him shelter and food.

"You will stay with your friend?"

"Probably."

"That does not make you happy?"

"No."

"He is not a good man?"

"He's a good man."

"But you are sad."

Ruth nodded. Hadad watched her tracing the wheel with one finger, round and round pointlessly. His arm remembered her head upon his shoulder. He watched and in time she looked up at him and again he saw the look of the deer drawing him to her.

"I cannot give to you. I have nothing. And I will die soon, on the mountain. But I have learned to want. I have learned to want you. Will you come with me into the mountains?"

Ruth looked down at her hands, and then slowly she shook her head from side to side.

"I don't deserve you, Hadad."

"I do not offer you anything. It is I who do not deserve."

"That's not true. You are brave. You are honest. You truly care about Earth ones even though they want to kill you. You work hard. You are compassionate. And . . . you . . . love me and I do not deserve your love. Hadad, you are everything I have ever wanted in a lover and I cannot live with you. I don't deserve you. I am not brave. I am selfish, and foolish, and I betray you and myself. And I am afraid of the mountains that you know. They are not the mountains I have lived in. And I am afraid of the death you accept so . . . passively. I want life. And everywhere around me there is death. Even with you."

The words came hard from her. Hadad watched as she spoke. But he did not hear her. For once he did not listen with his awareness. This time he did not hear her fears; he heard only his own. No longer was he human in appearance. The textured green skin on his chest was now exposed and showed through the holes in the shirt he wore. His face was scratched, even his hands were evident in the tears he had gotten in climbing. Only his feet, still booted, were smooth and plastic, pink and untextured. He was a lizard. And he was certain that though she would not say she found him repulsive, she must.

"Ruth, I cannot not be what I am."

He watched as she nodded. And then he reached in the backseat for another shirt to replace the one he wore, and a jacket to cover him further, and after he had put them on, he opened the door and got out of the car.

Ruth did not speak to stop him. He wasn't certain there were any words that she could say now that would make him change his mind. He closed the car door and walked back to the highway, crossed the road, and climbed to the ridge, not looking back.

Chapter 14

That the hover craft had been able to return to the mother ship at all was due only to Patricia's superb skill as a pilot. The lightning had damaged most of the electrical systems. They could not climb, and so she had maneuvered them down the canyon, past Mount Jefferson, and out over the plains, where they could land safely even if they could not maintain enough altitude to reach the mother ship. Once they were safely over the desert, she had rewired the console to get ignition to the rocket lifters. And with little power to spare, they had glided into the covered deck.

Eleanor was waiting in the hangar when they had cleared the decontamination system. Paul questioned whether he had been too lenient to release her from her quarters. Jeffrey had been pressing him too hard. He had not been able to answer all his accusations, and so he had released Eleanor on a scientific pretext, certain that once Jeffrey had his own avenue of authority, he would cease to probe, cease to accuse him of fifth-column activities. He had been right. As soon as Eleanor's guard had been removed, Jeffrey had been there demanding authority from her to raid the gorge. And she had conceded, just as Paul had known she would.

"We had given you up for dead, my dears. You have been away from the ship for four and a half hours. The antitoxin wore off at least two hours ago. But you seem healthy enough. I must have specimens. You've become my most noteworthy subjects."

152

"Forget your tests, Eleanor. We have been in a self-contained unit. All the air in the craft came from the mother ship. We have not tasted Earth's atmosphere this evening."

Paul lied. The air-duct system in the hover craft had been set to circulate with fresh air from the environment. He and the other fifth columnists on the ship carried ample supplies of resistance antitoxin from the Bates laboratories. They did not use Eleanor's concoction, and so he had not thought about the time limit he, too, must observe as commander. Now he could not risk Eleanor's probing. He left the hangar, headed toward his quarters. If Eleanor wanted to talk she would have to follow him. Patricia had already left the hangar and disappeared into the flight-crew quarters below.

"Has Jeffrey returned?"

"Your concern for him is touching, Paul."

"His well-being is not my concern, Eleanor. He had a mission. Self-appointed, I grant you, but a mission nonetheless. And as military commander, I am entitled to know its outcome."

"Of course."

They continued down the corridor. After about twenty yards, Paul turned and faced Eleanor, catching her arm to stop her.

"I asked a question, Eleanor. I am waiting for an answer."

She looked up at him, opened and closed her mouth, looked down at the floor, back up at him, and swallowed.

"Yes. He's back. He's wounded." She looked down at the floor again. "He was the only one who made it back."

"That doesn't surprise me. He ran into an ambush."

Her eyes flashed up at him. "How did you know?"

"I leave my radios on, Eleanor. He doesn't. He had plenty of warning from his point ship. Your 'Captain' is careless. And this time it's costing him his rank. We can't afford to squander fighter pilots to support his heroic gestures."

"The priest is dead."

"What makes you think so?"

"Jeffrey said no one escaped the fire."

"Jeffrey said."

"They couldn't land. They burned tne whole canyon. I think it is a fair assumption that the dissident priest perished in the flames."

"It might be a fair assumption. That does not make it a fact. We will see just how successful Jeffrey's mission really was. Good night, Eleanor."

The science officer stared at him. And then she left, turning down the corridor toward the medical support unit rather than toward her own quarters. *So she is going to report my reaction to Jeffrey!* Paul smiled. Tomorrow he would send a scout to find the car they had been following. He must know now if the priest had escaped the fire. He must contact him before Jeffrey gained strength to pursue his vendetta any further. Tomorrow.

Chapter 15

The sun cut across the morning rain and drew a rainbow over the green lake. The water was placid and each drop created a circle on the dark surface. Hadad sat in a tree on the northeast shore. The mountainsides were muddy. Snails and slugs rode on the slippery ground and ventured as far as the water would carry them. Hadad had taken his fill of the delicacy and then he had wandered back to the lake to watch the rain on the water.

He was tired, and cradled in the branches, hidden from the ground below, he slept.

"And they that recognize the light shall not see death."

The words echoed in his head as though a voice had spoken them in a deep and hollow chamber. He woke and looked around the lake. There was no one. People moved in the streets, yards behind him in the town, but there was no one near him, no one near the shore, no one who could have spoken the words.

He closed his eyes and tried to return to sleep.

"And they that recognize the light shall not . . ."

He opened his eyes quickly, but there was no one.

"Shall not see death." He completed the phrase aloud. He stared at the lake now reflecting the clear sky above, still green, deep green with the color of the trees that grew up the mountains that surrounded it.

". . . the death you accept so . . . passively; so . . . passively; so passively; so passively." Ruth's voice echoed in his mind.

He traced the bark on the branch that held him.

When had he begun to accept death passively?

He thought of his dream, of the nightmare that had come again and again, of the balloon chasing him with the red dust.

When had he accepted that death was inevitable?

Had it been when the red dust had been released? When he had been abandoned on the planet?

Each time he had moved he had anticipated death, waited for it, and it had not come. He had assumed he had escaped the red dust. But he had come so far into the mountains. For the first time he considered that he might have been wrong. Perhaps the high desert had been dusted. Perhaps the toxin was permeating the food supply he had been depending upon. Perhaps it had not affected him. But why?

"And they that recognize the light shall not see death."

The voice again. Where had he heard that voice? Why was he hearing it now?

"So passively." Ruth's accusation worked at him. Why did he accept death passively?

He closed his eyes, searching memory for some clue. Back he moved through the days at Vida, the months in Prineville, the weeks in Los Angeles, the years on the mother ship, the hours at The Leader's compound, the— He stopped. He had spent two years with The Leader, why did he remember only a few hours at the compound? He had been a child when the soldiers had taken him to The Leader; why did he remember some recruitment speech? He had not been recruited. And who was Jeffrey? He could not remember Jeffrey at home in his village. Why had he always thought of Jeffrey as a childhood friend?

"The Leader's is the cause for which I would die, but there is no cause for which I would kill." That was Diana's voice. Again and again, why was she repeating it again and again? Where was she? Why was he hearing her voice? The words, they were wrong. They were the wrong words.

"Say it, Gclixtchp. 'The Leader's is the cause for which I would die, but there is no cause for which I would kill.' Repeat the covenant, Gclixtchp. 'The Leader's is the cause for which I would die, but there is no cause for which I would kill.'"

No, those are the wrong words; that's not right." The child's voice he remembered as his own. But where was he? Where was the child? He could not remember where he had heard Diana's voice. She had to have been at the compound. He had been at the compound for two years. Why couldn't he remember those two years? Who was Jeffrey?

"This is your friend, Jeffrey. You have known him all your life. He is your friend. And he has grown up with you. Now you will join The Leader's cause together. You will be a king, and Jeffrey will be at your right hand forever; forever; forever." That was Diana's voice. What had her voice to do with . . . ? He had met Diana on the ship. He remembered being introduced. Meeting the—wait. He had met her on the ship. But she had looked familiar, like he had seen her before, but he couldn't remember where. Where had he met her before?

"Say the words, Gclixtchp. 'The Leader's is the cause for which I would die, but there is no cause for which I would kill.' Say the words, and I will make all the fire go away."

"But they aren't the right words."

"Say the words, Gclixtchp, and I will make all the fire go away."

The fire. What did she mean by "all the fire"? Where was the fire?

And then the fire surrounded him. There were flames everywhere. Flames that leaped out and burned at his lizard skin. Flames that consumed his mother, his father, tore at the house he had known as home. "The Leader's is the cause for which I would die, but there is no cause for which I would kill." That was his voice. He had said the words and the flames had disappeared. There had been no fire. His parents were still alive. He was just in a room, a room surrounded by glass. And there, beyond the glass, that's where he had seen her before! There, beyond the glass, was Diana!

Those were the wrong words. She had made him say them in the conversion chamber. He had believed them because she had made him believe them. But they were the wrong words.

What were the right words?

He closed his eyes hard against the light of the day around him. He tried hard to remember the words and they would not come to him. He tried hard to remember.

The leather was still wet against his skin. The day was warming, but the night's rains had soaked the legs of the deer that hid his own green flesh and the morning rains had soaked through the new jacket and the shoulders of the new shirt he wore. The rough leather lay against his shoulders like a yoke.

Like the ceremonial yoke that had been laid upon . . .

He had been seven, the time of . . . what were the words?

"Zon is the cause for which I would die, but there is no cause for which I would kill." The voice of his childhood spoke the words clearly in the hall of the elders. He remembered the candles, the white robes, the bands of gold.

"Of course! Zon teaches compassion. Zon is the cause for which I would die, not The Leader's cause. 'And they that recognize the light shall not see death.' The red dust doesn't kill me. It doesn't kill me. It's all around me and it doesn't kill me."

"I want life. And everywhere around me there is death. Even with you. Even with you. Even with . . ."

Now he could hear the words she had spoken earlier that he had closed away from his thoughts. She did not want to live with his preoccupation with death. It was that that had driven her away, not the lizardness that he had tried to deny and could not. He had to find her.

There was no one around and so he dropped to the ground rather than climb down the way an Earth one would. He walked back to the intersection. To turn to the right would take him back the way he had come from the mountains in the morning. He had not seen a ranger station there.

"Whatcha looking for, bud?" The voice came from the house to his left. He turned and saw the old man sitting by the window.

"A ranger station."

"Just go left there. On out to the highway. It's around on the north side of the lake. You can't miss it."

"Thank you."

"No problem."

He took off the jacket as he walked and let the warm noon sun dry the shoulders of his shirt. There were a few houses by the road, and smells of bread rising, clothes drying, diapers unchanged, soap, roses, identified themselves for Hadad as he passed.

The highway was edged by spruce and firs. Rhododendrons spread their broad leaf clusters to catch the sunlight, and ferns hid in the dark shade of the tall trees. The air was warm and mosquitoes investigated him as he walked.

The station was on his right, marked with a sign that rested on stone. He crossed the pavement marked for parked cars and climbed the steps. The door was locked and the office was empty. He pounded on the door, but no one answered.

A driveway wound up the hill to the west of the building. He walked back down the steps, and looking back over his shoulder at the deserted building in case anyone should answer his summons, he followed the pavement to the back. There behind the office building was a large open shed, its roof almost reaching the top of the aspens that grew beside it. There were vehicles parked all around the drive, green cars that bore the same emblem as the sign in front, trucks with long derricks that could raise a man to the treetops, flatbed trucks that bore the trimmings of the forest around him, a bulldozer, and beyond, a truck with hoses wrapped in long coils. There was no one in the driveway or around the trucks.

To the left of the drive were houses behind a hedge of blackberries. A gray-and-white one faced the road, above it a green one faced the driveway, beyond that another green one nestled in the trees. Hadad walked toward the gray-and-white house and then saw Ruth's car in the driveway beyond the farthest green one. He walked toward it.

The voices came to him clearly from the house before he reached it. He recognized the woman's voice as Ruth's.

"That's not the point."

"How can it not be the point?"

"You say it's my baby."

"Are you contesting it?"

"Well, if it's my baby, then I should have some say over whether it gets born into this crazy world or not."

"It's not your responsibility."

"How can you say it isn't?"

"I'm not asking you to be responsible."

"You just walked in here and asked if you can stay. I

suppose the next thing you are going to tell me is that you aren't asking me to be responsible for your well-being either."

"I'm not."

"Ruth, you can't have it both ways."

"Ron, I've been driving all night; everything I own except the leather and the car went up in flames; I've been shot at by lizards and almost struck by lightning. I need a roof over my head and a refuge and you have the audacity to say I'm welcome as long as I'm not pregnant. Especially with your child."

"Which I said I didn't want in the first place."

"I'm not saying you said you wanted it. I'm only saying I won't take the responsibility for taking its life."

"Ruth, you don't want that child either."

"That's beside the point."

"No, that is the point."

"No, it's not."

"Ruth, we are living on the edge of time. We could die at any moment ourselves."

"My point exactly."

"I can't see how you've even looked at that. There's no food coming into the mountains. There hasn't been for weeks. We're stuck with what we have on the shelves and what we can grow in the fields. And we aren't farmers, Ruth. We're having to learn it all from scratch. You came here because there wasn't anywhere else you could go. Okay, then you get to rake and hoe with the rest of us. You're another mouth to feed. That's all you are. And as far as I'm concerned, that's already one too many. But you're talking about two mouths to feed. And I don't want to be responsible for that second one."

"It's not as though the planet is overrun with people, Ron. More than a third of the inhabitants of the planet have been taken by the lizards already."

"And the rest of us are going to get starved out, or wiped out by infection, or burned out, or shot, unless we can find ways to survive on our own. Ruth, the only reason we're making it here is water. We've got water. This planet is starving for water and we've got it at our doorstep. But we haven't got anything else going for us. You didn't need to come back. If you had enough gas to get here, you could have gotten down into the valley. Why didn't you go there?"

"I couldn't."

"Why not?"

"Someone was with me."

"Who?"

"A friend."

"Another person here in Detroit. Another mouth to feed."

"You won't have to worry about that."

"Maybe not personally, but we're all in this together. You haven't gotten that yet. You still think it's unlimited supply and demand. You're crazy, Ruth. You're living in a fantasy world. The rules have changed. It's dog eat dog. And it may come to that with the lizards on one side of us and the army camped on the other."

"Ron, your priorities are backward."

"And I stopped worrying about your approval when you left me. I look out for me and mine, and that doesn't include you anymore."

Hadad took the steps to the house two at a time.

"I don't know what made me think you'd care."

"I don't either. I've got other worries now, Ruth. I'm a ranger. There are people I care about in Detroit, and we've got lizards on our doorstep. Your concerns just don't reach me anymore."

Hadad rapped on the door.

And then he heard the hover craft. He dove past the window and off into the woods and laser fire slashed across the door and the front of the house, trailed him across the vegetable garden, and bit into the trees behind him. He ran as scattered a course as he could manage, breaking his stride, cutting first to the left, then to the right. There was a culvert about a mile behind the station, and he dove into it and ran its length before moving back into the trees again.

The hover craft pursued him, dove past him, circled back, and tried to cut him off. He doubled back, and then began to climb as the craft cut his path again.

And then he tripped the snare. It was a simple woodsman's trap, set for deer or coyote. The rope closed around his ankle and lifted him twenty feet into the air. And to the hover craft it must have seemed that he disappeared. The firing continued along the path he had been running, and then it stopped. The craft circled, and then it stopped, and then it moved away beyond the mountain, east past the village.

He had heard Ruth scream his name as he ran past the window. He had to get back to her.

He doubled his body up to the rope and then climbed, hand over hand, until he reached the branch. Once he had his other leg over the limb, he could untie his bound ankle.

He climbed down the tree so that he could pull the snare with him. And carefully he reset it, using the same rocks that had held it before.

When the snare was set, he walked back down the mountain, cutting straight across the firebreaks and gardens to the ranger's house.

The house was silent.

Hadad climbed the stairs and knocked again.

A man opened the door and stared at him, twisting his cheek as he examined Hadad's torn face.

"What do you want?"

"Is Ruth here?"

"No such luck. She went for a walk."

"Where does she walk?"

"Same place we all do around here." The man gestured toward the road. "Try the park."

The man closed the door, and Hadad looked to see where he had pointed. There was a path between the trees that led down to the road. He followed it. From there he could see a driveway leading from the highway down to the lake shore. He crossed the road and cut through the trees, down past the campsites, where boxes delineated territory and tents provided protection, and furnishings from homes long ago abandoned shaped the space between trees into a memory of something called home.

There was a road between the campsites, and markers numbering the sites. He walked, trying not to disturb the walls of air that defined the privacy of each family, seeking in a passing glance the whereabouts of Ruth. She was not in the campground.

He walked back along the trees that edged the long stretch of sand reaching down to the water's edge. He searched the sand and found the only Earth ones. There was a mother and her son, about four years old, who were playing along the water's edge. He passed them, walking east, reached the end of the campgrounds without finding Ruth, and turned back, retracing his steps along the tree-lined edges of the camps.

He spotted her down beyond the bay that marked the end of state park sites, walking back from the boat ramp at the far west end of the beach. He stopped and watched her walking, knowing she could not see him.

He watched as she watched the sand, then looked out at the water, ahead at trees, up at the sky, back to the sand at her feet. He moved out from the trees, out onto the sand, walking deliberately, slowly, toward her, unsure of how she would greet him, aware of the argument that worried her, knowing she did not know he had heard it. Knowing she did not know whether he had lived or had died as he ran from the hovercraft fire. He watched her, unaware of him, and he saw the moment she recognized him coming toward her. And then he had no doubts. In the moment of recognition she began to run toward him, and so he, too, ran, toward her.

There were still yards between them when he heard the hover craft returning. It was behind him, and so he turned and ran back toward the forest, and the shots intended for him dug a trench in the hard sand. The craft passed, and he ran back to the sand and saw Ruth lying facedown beyond him.

"Ruth!" He wailed her name, certain that she had been shot by the craft as it strafed the ground.

He saw her get to her feet and he wailed again, this time in relief.

And then he saw the craft was not turning. Out beyond the boat ramp, down between the narrowing canyon walls it continued, and then it opened fire.

He had not traveled that end of the lake. But he had seen the other fingers, where water fed in flowing torrents toward the still, green waters, tumbled freely over rocks in waterfalls, gushed from mountain streams down to bridgeworthy rivers to fill this great chasm in the mountains. The rivers were rapid, the lake still and deep. At the far end there had to be a dam holding all of this in check.

To his left, perhaps a hundred yards away, the four-year-old played in the water, his mother encouraging him to paddle to her, to swim.

Hadad turned from Ruth and ran to the water's edge. Now he ran faster than he had from the hover craft, faster than he had when pursued by Jerry, faster than he had in the dream. As he ran he heard the explosions—one, two, three, four—and then the slow rush of water began.

He passed the mother and knocked her back onto the sand, but the child was already being pulled away from the shore. He dove into the water and swam with the suction out into the lake.

The child dropped beneath the surface, and for a moment Hadad did not know where he was, and then he came up farther away. He swam faster and finally caught the boy. But the child was frightened, as much of him as of the sucking water, and he struggled to be free of the clenching hand that held him.

Hadad could not swim against the pull of the water, and so he rode across the current and aimed for the boat ramp at the far end of the beach. The child no longer struggled, but the water was strong and tried to pull him away from the shore, out farther into the trench of water headed for the dam. He pulled against the water. The shore raced past. He could not reach the boat ramp. It was still too far to the right. Now he aimed for the trees between the ramp and the turn of the shore. First the nearest, and then when that seemed out of reach, the one beside it.

He grabbed for the root of an oak just as the shore threatened to recede on the other side of the point. It held. And so he gripped it, and held to it as the water dragged across his body, down his arm, pulling on the child he held with his other hand. The boy's head bobbed beneath the surface. He had not resisted for so many yards, Hadad feared that he had drowned as he had pulled him through the water. He tried now to pull the child to him, but the water held them stretched from the shore.

And then the water receded from the shallows and the two swimmers lay upon the wet sand.

Hadad pulled the child to him and laid him across his leg, rhythmically he pressed the water from the boy's stomach, and then he turned him to himself and put his mouth over the boy's mouth and breathed into him. His hands felt the pressure points in the back of the boy's neck and on his chest. There was energy there, weak but present, and so Hadad pressed on the vital points and drew the energy of Zon down into the life of the child.

Chapter 16

The boy opened his eyes as his mother and Ruth reached them on the sand.

"Oh, Johnny, oh, how can I thank you, oh, thank God you're all right, how can I thank you, oh, my God." The words washed over them as the mother gathered up the child and held him to her. Her feet were bleeding where they had been cut on the stones she'd crossed running to them, but she didn't notice.

The craft had continued firing as Hadad had struggled for shore. He had heard the explosions. He did not know what they had meant. There had not been time to consider what they might have meant. Now, as the emergency drew away from his awareness, there was left the curiosity, the concern.

He felt Ruth's hands on his arm. He wanted now the greeting that he had missed short minutes before, but it was not there. She tugged at his arm and shouted though he was there beside her.

"They will be back. We have to get off the beach. Get up. Don't just sit there. Don't you see; they will be back any minute. Get up. Please get up."

The words did not hold meaning. His body was tired. His being ached for solace. But the urgency in her voice drove him to his feet. She was there. They were together. And now, as on the road in Vida, he trusted without question.

They ran across the widening sand. She urged him to run faster, but the weariness was pouring through his body and the trees seemed distant and unreachable.

"Come back. You must let me thank you. You must let me do something. I don't even know your name. How can I thank you?" the mother of the child shouted after them. Hadad turned back at her cry and saw her, holding the child, out behind the line of trees, out alone, a promontory against the rushing water.

"Hadad, run."

"Ruth, I can't."

"You must. Don't talk. Just run."

And then he saw the source of her concern.

The hover craft came back up the shore line. It flew low and slowly, giving the pilot plenty of time to search the edges of the forest for movement, for any sign of him.

The woman was still shouting at him, still clutching her child and shouting for him to return. He could no longer hear her shouts, no longer hear anything but the drone of the craft. And movement, all movement, appeared to slow and distort into nightmare, for there was nothing he could do.

He shouted.

"No" wrenched from him, torn from the sinews of his back, from the tendons of his legs, from the marrow of his spine.

He saw the light as the weapons on the ship fired.

He saw the moment move toward him as if it were a tangible thing moving through space.

He saw the woman's face as death reached her, though she was too far behind them now for any clarity to be possible. He saw it clearly as the agony spread through her. He saw the despair engulf her. And then he realized that the child she carried was already dead. And he watched as she fell lifeless on the sand.

He ran.

Ruth was a few steps ahead of him. They crossed the boat ramp and ran into the trees. The craft traced with fire the path they had run.

Again he was running. The scattered limbs from trees, the leaves of bushes, worn dirt paths, and hard black road surfaces seemed unreal to him. Again he was running. It would be so easy to stop, to give in to the death that pursued him.

The Leader's is the cause for which I would die, but there is no cause for which I would kill.

It would serve The Leader for him to die. He could so easily just step out onto the sand and wait for death.

"Run, Hadad." Ruth's voice pulled at him from the road ahead.

The Leader's is the cause for which I would die . . .

"Hadad, come on."

The cause for which . . . so passively . . . so passively.

"Run, will you? Hadad, please!"

Not the right words, no, what were the right words?

"Over here, lady."

"We can't stop."

"He's in no shape to run. Get in the camper. They can't see you through those trees. I'll say you ran past. Get him in here. He's about to drop."

There were rough hands on his left arm, soft ones on his right. Steps rose under his feet and there were metal strips that brushed his shoulders and then it was warmer yet than the air warmed by the sun and then there was softness on his cheek and then he no longer stood upon the world.

Darkness. Red-brown darkness.

A key turned in a lock.

Not the right words.

Pressure moved over his body like liquid. Orange consuming darkness.

Say the words and I'll make all the fire go away. Say the words. Say the words. Say the words. Say the words.

"Oh, my God, they're landing."

Say the words . . . not the right words . . . say the words . . . not the right words . . . the right words . . . the right words.

A helmet fit down over his head. It was soft and clung to his temples. His body was tossed into the void and fell down, down, down to the yellow pit of darkness.

You are to be a king . . . a king . . . a king . . . and Jeffrey will always be at your right hand . . . hand . . . hand.

Something pulled his left arm away from his body and stretched it out into space. It floated from him, never leaving him, extending out into swirls of space, of water, of space, of water, clutching the child bobbing beneath the water.

"No, open your hand, put it through here."

Clutching the child.

"Hadad, open your hand. Please do as I say."

Do as I say the words . . . not the right words . . . as I say . . . as I say.

Something opened his hand and the child slipped away in the water, and his arm moved through a silky tunnel into space and the tunnel folded down around him, covering his shoulders so that his arm and body were no longer there in space. Only his hand was there in space, in the yellow space. Only his hand and his head in the tight, soft helmet floated in the yellow pit of space.

"Spread out. They have to be here somewhere. Search the campsites. You. Is this your camper?"

"There's no one in there but my wife. She's ill."

"Open the door."

"She's a sick woman."

"Open the door."

"I can't let you disturb her."

Explosion ripped the yellow space and triangular

chips of yellow cut into the tunnel that covered his
body. Man-scream ripped the darkness and he fell
forward through the seam of space into clutching,
binding, mottled greenness.

He moaned.

"Shhhhhhhh."

Steam filled the green darkness.

Gears ground as the steam surrounded him and the
fabric of space shook.

"It's locked."

"Shoot the lock."

Lightning flashed across the mottled green canopy
of space and became a net of lace that closed around
him, moving toward him to cover him, his head, his
hands, his face, with green-white lace.

"What a stench in there."

"Check it out."

"Just his wife there in the bed, like he said."

"I said check it out."

Hammers pounded on the crystallized lace around
his head and broke it into shards.

"I've had enough of human stink. There's nobody
here."

"Try the next one."

The gap in space closed with a click. And air
escaped from a valve beside him and the green
balloon of space closed around him, covering him in
tight, binding green rubber. Something pulled the
rubber away from his face, stripped it back from his
body, pulled the helmet from his head, took the
tunnel from his arm and torso, stripped away all that
held him, and lifted his body up into the light-blue
darkness.

"Hadad?"

Explosions became small stars in the light-blue
firmament. And as they streaked across the sky they

wailed, falling through to nothingness, evaporating in the blue.

"Oh, my God, they're shooting up the camp. They are killing everyone. Oh, Hadad."

You will be a king. And your name will be Hadad. For you will rebuild the city of Pau and the people of Earth will follow you as they did the great king of the desert. And you will teach them the truths of The Leader. The Leader teaches surrender. The Leader teaches acceptance of his ways. The Leader teaches obedience to his plan. You will witness to the people of Earth that all life comes from The Leader. The hand of The Leader is everywhere. Now, Gclixtchp, say the words of the covenant: The Leader's in the cause for which I would die, but there is no cause for which I would kill. Say the words.

"No." The word reverberated through the blue universe and echoed in the cells of his body.

Something descended through the blue, closer, closer. It pressed down upon his chest, moved down toward his face, and then touched only his lips. Space itself kissed him and yielded up itself to him in its resplendent cobalt-blue, star-studded wonder.

"I love you, Hadad."

"Zon teaches compassion." The voice came from the fullness of the cosmos. *"Speak the words of the covenant, my son."* The voice permeated all that was; and the voice within him responded slowly, deliberately, confidently: *Zon is the cause for which I would die, but there is no cause for which I would kill.*

He floated then among the stars. There were explosions around him as stars were born and died. Sirens wailed as comets swung through solar rings, and shots crackled as starchildren went supernova—the cosmic celebration of the Lords of Light.

Hadad opened his eyes. Ruth sat beside him, looking at him. He was not certain where he was. There were brown metal walls around him; he lay in a bed; clothes were scattered around the room, clothes he had never seen before. Beyond the metal walls men ran through the forests. He could hear them as they passed. There were shots and shouts.

"Behind you!" Another shot.

"Okay, cover me!" A barrage of rifle fire.

"Over here." The whistle of approaching death. The choke of pain, of injury.

"They got me, Ron. You take over. Drive them back to that ship of theirs."

"All right, men. Push 'em back."

Heavy fire. Running.

More.

And then the whine of the hover craft.

And then the silence.

Boots thudded on the ground as the rangers moved back from the beach into the campground.

"We're gonna need the bulldozer to clean up this mess. Bob, take Jack back to the station. See to his leg, then get the dozer and bring it down here. We might as well bury this place; there's bodies all over. Shit. Okay, men. Let's see if we've got any survivors."

"Ruth, what has happened?" Hadad spoke very quietly.

"The Visitors attacked the camp."

"They were looking for me."

"Yes."

"And the Earth ones?"

"The campers are dead."

"And who are the voices?"

"The rangers drove the Visitors back to the hover craft. They're gone now."

"The voice that says what to do? That is your friend?"

"Yes."

Hadad watched Ruth's face for grief, for fear, for anger. He saw only concern. She reached toward him and stroked his face with her fingers, tracing the places where the human covering had ripped.

"You need your medicine plant."

"It will have to heal slowly. Some of the places are badly torn. There is not enough to grow back, to cover the flesh that is mine."

He reached a hand toward her, green, traced with lines dark beneath the surface that carried the dark translucent liquid to his fingers.

She took his hand and ran her hand over it. He could feel her touch. And he looked up to feel the touch of her eyes.

The door of the camper opened suddenly and the man Hadad had seen at the house stared in at them. His breath snorted out as his face twisted and he looked down at the ground.

"I might have known."

He came into the camper and looked around, brushed aside a shirt that lay on the bench beside the table and sat down across from them. Hadad still lay on the bed. Ruth sat beside him, though she turned her body now to face the man.

"They were after him, weren't they?"

"Yes."

"I am wanted by my . . ."

"Look, mister, I don't know who you are, but I don't want to hear it. I'm only interested in what she has to say."

"I'm sorry, Ron."

"That's not good enough. You hid him in here while seventy-five people, seventy-five innocent people who don't even know you, all died. For no reason, they all died. I can't figure out why they didn't find you. Didn't they open the door? Or did you hide in here someplace?"

"One of them came in. The man . . . the man who hid us here had said his wife was sick in here. I guess he convinced them. They were here. They went on."

"That doesn't make sense. They even killed a baby in a playpen, and they just walked past the two of you. I don't get it. Who is he anyway? What makes him so special?"

"This is my friend, Ha—David."

Hadad knew that the custom of Earth ones was to shake hands. But he did not want to extend his hand to this man. Lying on his leg, behind Ruth's back, the bare hand would not betray him. His face was cut, but none was torn away. The sleeves of the shirt hid his arms, the pants and boots, his legs. Only his hands were evidence against him. He did not move.

"Forgive me if I don't say I'm pleased to meet you. But I'm not. We were doing okay here. We had water. We had places for people to live. We were growing food. We were gonna make it. And here in the mountains they'd never have spotted us. Now we're a prime target. What do they want him for, anyway?" He directed the question back to Ruth.

Hadad waited for her answer. He wondered how she would interpret this strange chase. He had not known himself before why the ships pursued him. He had assumed it was because he had angered Diana while he was on the ship. Now he understood it was more than that. Diana had converted him for The Leader. And then she had distrusted the idea of his exercising authority that might rival hers. And so she had taken away first the power, then the authority, finally the desire to live.

When he had not died, she had ordered him killed.

He knew now that the power of Zon within him was stronger than Diana's influence had been.

He wondered what Ruth would say.

"He was to be a king. In another country. He was

ousted in a political struggle. The Visitors have converted or deposed all the political leaders they've been able to find. They want to use his influence against his own people."

Hadad listened as she made up the story out of the bits and pieces of what he had shared with her. She did not lie. And nothing she said betrayed the truth.

"He can't stay here. As long as they think he's here, they'll be back."

"They may come back anyway. Even if we go."

"I was hoping that wasn't obvious except in my mind. Ruth, we can't hide him here forever. They will kill off all of us to find him. And eventually they *will* find him. I can only hope they're following your car. That's the only hope there is for Detroit, Oregon. If he's that important to them, our lives here are worthless. They'll wipe us out one way or the other. They blew up both of the dams. We're trapped here, Ruth. The Visitors are east of us, and the road down to Salem is under water. Get him out of here. And don't come back. I don't want to see you again."

"I don't know where to go, Ron. We're just as trapped as you are."

"You still don't see it, do you? It's the same as with the baby. You can't see the big picture. Ruth, sometimes it's necessary for one person to die so that others can live. Take him to the Visitors. Let them have *him* so they'll leave the rest of us alone. I'll have Jay take you back to the station. Take the car and get out of here."

"I haven't enough gas."

"We'll fill the tank for you. Just get him out of here."

The ranger pushed himself away from the narrow seat, away from the table. He looked at Hadad and then at Ruth. He shook his head and then he left the camper.

"Jay. Take a car and run these folks back to the station. Ruth's car is in my driveway. Make sure she's got a tank of gas. They're heading east. Make sure they get out of town."

The man named Jay stuck his head through the doorway.

"Okay, folks. It's safe to come out now. The Visitors have gone. We'll get you on your way. It's okay."

Ruth glanced at Hadad and then got up from the bed and moved toward the doorway. Hadad swung his legs to the side of the bed and checked his clothing. The leathers were damp, but not torn. Only his hands were exposed. And he had no pockets. He glanced around the camper. Clothes were tossed everywhere. He rummaged through a drawer, nothing. Then a basket of what had possibly been laundry. There were no gloves there. He was about to give up when he saw the leather work gloves tucked just inside the door. He grabbed them and put them on quickly.

"Hey, fella, c'mon." Jay came back to the doorway.

"I am coming."

The man nodded, and Hadad finished putting on the other glove and followed.

The rangers had pulled the bodies to the edge of the campground. There they lay in a stack, Visitors and Earth ones thrown together by chance, indistinguishable except for the color of their clothes.

The bulldozer passed them on the boat ramp as they went back up the highway in the ranger's car.

"You sure you folks have to leave Detroit? Seems you'd be a lot safer sticking around here than driving off into those mountains. You're gonna encounter an armed roadblock out on twenty-two."

"We have to go, Jay. It's best."

"Whatever you say. Ruth, I don't know what happened with you and Ron. He was real upset when you left."

"It's okay, Jay. It's over, that's all."

"I'm real sorry about that."

"Thanks. You've been a good friend."

They rode in silence the rest of the way back to the station.

Hadad watched the trees as they flicked past the car.

Ruth pulled the car over to the driveway by the shed that sheltered the forestry vehicles. Jay pumped the gas into the car for her and then waved as they drove down the driveway to the highway and turned east.

"Good, he isn't going to escort us out of town."

"Why is that good?"

"Because we're not going east. We're going north. There's a resort up in the mountains. We're going there."

"No, Ruth. More people will be killed. Ron is right. Take me back to the desert."

"No, Hadad. He's not right. I saw what they did to Prineville. They'll do that to Detroit whether they find you or not."

"But the place in the mountains. The people there. I cannot run forever."

"There aren't any people there. We were talking about it this morning. All the people came down to Detroit. They're helping to organize the village, make it self-sufficient. They were some of the people who taught me healing. Now they're teaching the folks how to raise the right kind of food."

"And you. You cannot live without food."

"Hadad, the mountains feed *you*."

"Yes."

"Then they will feed me too."

Chapter 17

Paul lay in the tub surrounded by bubbles.

He expected Patricia.

He had been at the console all afternoon examining contour maps, comparing population-density maps with his terrain analysis. The populations of the Central Oregon towns were almost all stored aboard. The antitoxin was adequate for his purposes and the purgatives seemed to detoxify the food specimens adequately so that they did not poison the diners at his table.

The Oregon project was just about complete. Now the rest of the Earth's population, that beyond reach before, would be fair game. He had spent the afternoon plotting the most advantageous move in his struggle for power.

He needed a major victory, a strategic masterpiece, one that would rival Diana's negotiation of the open city, best her in manipulation of Earth's leaders, demonstrate that victory was possible even without the conversion techniques, challenge her influence at the council, reveal the weaknesses that he had studied so carefully from her bed.

The work on the antitoxin had been his idea. The limit in its development had been his too. Full access to the planet without restraint for the entire fleet did not serve him. There were other commanders whose loyalties to Diana were stronger. He did not want to share his territory, his access to power, with them.

He calculated carefully his next move. He needed to pick a key position, one that would give him leverage in the political maneuverings that would come, even if he had to engineer them himself. He calculated a year. In a year his voice would frighten Diana as hers had intimidated him so many times. His voice would lead the rest of the ships, complete the transformation of Earth to the puppet state The Leader had so neatly designed. His choices would stay to govern Earth as he led home the victorious fleet. And his decision would make or break the careers and lives of those who saw him now as merely an extension of Diana's power.

His shoulders ached. He turned on the jets and sank down into the water to let the pulsing water ease the tensions of his concentration.

Water.

He had learned to enjoy the luxury of having it in plentiful supply. He reminded himself to check the ship's storage tanks in the morning. There were lakes in the mountains that would serve to replenish the supply if need be. He did not ever want to be again without water to spare.

He closed his eyes and let the rhythm of the pulsing jets soothe away the concerns of the day.

Images of Diana danced in front of him. Diana enticing him with a succulent mouse. Diana watching him at the console. Diana inviting him with a look. And Diana pulling him to her bed. Diana lying beneath him, waiting. He would keep her waiting.

This time it was Patricia who waited.

The water had cooled, and he was bored with the bubbles.

He stepped from the bath and wrapped himself in a robe of terry cloth that draped him and hung from his shoulders clear to the floor. He pulled up the hood and dried his head and then, comfortably dry, he dropped the robe and took a lighter garment that hung loosely from his shoulders.

Patricia stood by the door of his bedroom as he emerged.

"The craft has returned, sir."

"Good. What did they find?"

"They found the car where you said it would be."

"And the passengers?"

"The priest was there, sir. In Detroit, as you predicted."

"Good. I want Justine to contact him. He is obviously part of the resistance. We need to know how they are organized here in Oregon. They need our help. The processing operations have gone too smoothly. I expected more disruptions than the crews have experienced."

"Sir. It won't be as simple as that."

"And why not, my dear?"

"Sir. The craft was followed."

"Followed? By whom?"

"By another craft, sir."

"Jeffrey again?"

"No, sir. He is still under medical surveillance. But it would seem that the orders were his. The craft you sent was not aware it was being followed until after it had spotted the car. They followed the path we had taken, crossed the mountains, and then followed the road past the lake."

"Lake?"

"Yes, sir. There was a big lake on the other side of the ridge, beyond where we encountered the storm."

"Good. That will serve well. We can use more water aboard, I'm sure."

"I'm sorry, sir."

"What about?"

"It's not there."

"I beg your pardon."

"The lake is not there, sir."

"I think I'm a bit confused. Suppose you just come

over here with me and tell me the whole story. My questions don't seem to be clarifying anything."

He took Patricia's hand and led her to the bed. He dropped the tunic he had put on and spread out on the sheepskin.

"The shoulders, Patricia. Be a dear."

Fully uniformed, Patricia knelt onto the bed and straddled his body. Her hands worked the muscles of his back as she talked.

"The scouts went out this morning. They headed south toward Bend, as you had suggested, to avert suspicion. And then they turned up into the mountains. They didn't bother to follow the gorge. I had given them the exact location of where the lightning had struck us."

"Of course. Down a little lower."

"Sir?"

"A little lower on the left."

"Yes, sir. Anyway, they followed the road down toward the village and started looking for the car. And they found it. They were turning back when they spotted the other craft, sir."

"The one that had followed them."

"Yes, sir. No one in the other craft would have recognized the car, sir. I had told only Justine what it looked like. It would have been easy to explain the venture as a search for water. There was a lake."

"Yes, you said that."

"I'm sorry, sir. I didn't mean to repeat myself."

"You said 'it would have been easy to explain.' That suggests that it no longer is."

"No, sir. I mean, yes, sir. I mean . . . the priest was standing in the parking lot near the car, sir. The other craft spotted him and recognized him and opened fire, sir. They chased him back into the hills, where he disappeared, sir."

"Then we'll search for him there."

"That isn't all, sir."

"Patricia, just tell me what happened."

"Justine turned back then. She was hoping the other craft would follow her, but it didn't. They circled, apparently looking for him, but they didn't find him, at least not right away, sir. It's not real clear why they destroyed the dam, sir."

"They destroyed a dam?"

"The one that held the lake, sir. For that matter, they destroyed two dams, sir."

"Two dams?"

"The one that held the lake, and the lower one as well."

"And no one knows why?"

"No, sir. According to Justine, it seemed more like a prank, sir."

"And so the priest is in the hills and a lake has been drained as a prank."

"Not quite, sir."

"There's more?"

"Yes, sir. After the dams had been destroyed, the craft went back past the town and they spotted the priest and a girl running along the shore. They opened fire, sir. But they missed him. And so they landed, sir."

"They what?"

"They landed, sir. And searched the campground where he was hiding."

"And they found him?"

"No, sir. But according to the stories the survivors are telling, they killed a hundred or more people while they were searching for him."

"The survivors?"

"Yes, sir. There were four survivors."

"Dare I ask how many casualties?"

"Six, sir."

"Ten soldiers just happened to be following the

scout ship in a ship of their own, blew up two dams for a prank, and managed with only six casualties to wipe out a population of over a hundred Earthlings. And miss the target they were aiming for."

"Yes, sir."

"I hope you're going to tell me they were a motley crew thrown together from Jeffrey's friends, and not my best soldiers."

"No, sir."

"Does that mean 'No, they were not his friends,' or 'No, they were not my best soldiers'?"

"No, they were not all his friends, sir."

"I see."

"That's not all, sir."

"There's more?"

"Park rangers opened fire on the landing crew. The casualties, sir. That's why. The rest got back to the craft and came back to the ship, sir. That's how we found out they hadn't found the priest and the girl."

"So he's somewhere in the campground or the forests or Detroit."

"No, sir. Justine and the other crew were still in the air when the other craft came back. She had decided to circle, to make sure they got away. She knew better than to leave a craft on the ground if they'd all been killed, sir. She would have gone back to blow it up."

"Yes, of course."

"That's how she happened to be there when the car left Detroit, sir."

"The car left Detroit?"

"Yes, sir. It went north. Up to some cabins in the hills. The girl and the priest are there. In the hills, sir."

"Then we know where they are?"

"Yes, sir."

"And Justine can contact him."

"If you wish, sir."

"Good."

He raised up on one elbow and Patricia moved back to sit on her heels at the foot of the bed. He stretched.

"That feels real good. Now to get you out of that uniform."

"Not yet, sir. You're expected on the bridge in ten minutes, sir."

"I am?"

"To speak to Diana as you arranged with her, sir."

"I made no arrangement to speak to Diana."

"It has been arranged, sir. It was assumed you had made the arrangement yourself."

"All right, I'll see to Diana. Will I see you later?"

"If you wish, sir."

"I wish."

Patricia smiled, and then she got to her feet and left. Paul laughed. "I wish. I do indeed wish."

He dressed in his uniform, snapped on the video monitor of his room, and went to the bridge.

Jeffrey was standing by the communications screen.

"I assume I owe this honor in some way to you, Jeffrey."

"I beg your pardon."

"You should. It was presumptuous of you to contact Diana. I trust you will have a casualty report for me from your little debacle today."

"News travels fast."

"You have some explaining to do."

"We'll see who ends up explaining."

Paul raised an eyebrow, and then turned to the screen.

The image of Diana appeared and the monitor assured him that she saw their images as well.

"Well, Paul. I'm surprised to hear from you."

"And I to be contacting you."

"What is the concern?" Her tone dropped the intimacy and became abruptly harsh.

"Perhaps we should allow Jeffrey to speak for himself, Diana."

"If he has something to say, of course. What is it, Jeffrey?"

"We have been in pursuit of the king-to-be, Hadad."

"Pursuit?" Diana's face held its calm, never betraying surprise, though Paul realized that she must have been surprised from her subsequent reaction. "I had thought he was dead. You know what you're to do, Jeffrey."

"Yes, Diana. *I* know what I'm to do. But there seems to be some question of authority."

"I have given a general order for the elimination of all the priests. They speak foolishness and disturb the troops with their talks of passivity and acceptance. Eliminate him. What else do you need to know?"

"Diana, that is your general order. But what about the specific order? As I say, there is a question of authority. I know the order that *I* carry concerning Hadad. But our illustrious military strategist has some other ideas. I defer to your judgment, Diana."

"What are these ideas he refers to, Paul?"

"Diana, Jeffrey has attempted to take over the whole operation of pursuit with regard to the priest. He has succeeded in missing him in three attempts, eliminating Earthlings that could have been processed, and wasting water that could have been pumped to augment the supplies on the ship. And he has lost track of Hadad's whereabouts in the process. I have no intention of turning over the military operations of this ship to him, or consulting him on the strategies I have planned. Is that clear?"

"Perfectly. The priest will be eliminated."

"The priest need not concern you, Diana."

"Exactly. Jeffrey, I release you from your life bond to Hadad. Since your superior has chosen to take the responsibility for his death, he shall be accountable. Do we understand each other?"

"Yes, Diana," Jeffrey answered, and looked up at Paul.

For a moment Paul was not certain he had won. He had not known about a life bond to Hadad. What had she referred to? One thing was certain: The priest must die, or Paul must pay for the negligence with his life.

"Paul? Do we understand each other?"

"Yes, Diana."

"Good. Is that all?"

"For now."

"Until the next time, then."

"Until then."

The image disappeared. Jeffrey watched him.

"You may rest assured, Jeffrey. I know where he is. And he will die. And you may even watch him die. You deserve that, at least. But you will send no one from this ship without my orders. Is that clear?"

"Yes, sir."

"You may return to your duties. On the ship."

"Yes, sir."

The junior officer left the bridge.

Justine was duty officer of the day. *How convenient,* Paul reflected.

"Justine. Bring me the duty rosters for the next seventy-two hours."

"Yes, sir." The tall brunette handed him the computer pad. The inoculation schedules were recorded there for all the ground crews and the military support personnel.

He noted the names of those marked deceased. He had lost good men. Seven other names were on seventy-two-hour hold. Justine's was among them.

"Three days." He looked at her, and she nodded. He would outline the plan to Patricia. This time

Justine would follow his directions. He smiled.

He returned to his quarters. Automatically he reached to switch the video monitor to prerecorded images to cover Patricia's return, but something stopped him.

He set the machine to scan the last half hour. There was nothing unusual for twenty minutes or so of real time. And then the source of his concern appeared on the screen. Eleanor.

She had entered without difficulty, though he knew he had scrambled the code on the interleaving doorway as he left for the bridge. She had searched his room very thoroughly and carefully. He tried to reason through her actions what she was searching for.

"You needn't worry. I found what I wanted," her voice came from behind him, from his bath.

He turned, expecting to find her in full uniform. Instead, she was wrapped in one of the terry robes he kept by his tub.

"I see you've made yourself at home, my dear."

"I thought under the circumstances you might prefer I take that privilege to some other."

"Intimacy becomes you. What did you have in mind?"

She walked slowly, seductively, toward him. She reached up with her right hand and stroked his head, tracing small circles with a single finger down behind his ear, down his neck, down to the collar of his uniform.

"I think, most properly, it's called blackmail, Paul."

"How charming. Are you sure you're up to it, Eleanor?"

"It hardly requires effort."

"Then it seems to me you must want something very much. I can't imagine what that might be."

He watched her reaction. His approach had thrown

her. She had expected him to question her about what she had found. He knew she would tell him in time, her time. There was no need to ask.

The seduction took a different tack. She moved away from him, casually strolled the room, as if assessing it for future investment.

"I want power, Paul. And an end to these petty struggles between us. I don't think our aims are so far apart. You need the prestige of my accomplishments. I need the authority of your position. We can work together. Or I can destroy you. It's as simple as that."

"Nothing is ever as simple as that, Eleanor."

"I've opened the temperate zones of Earth to you, Paul. Your next step is to organize part of the fleet, under your control, of course, and recapture the colder cities of the world. You've already planned the operation. Oh, don't look so surprised. I've seen the maps you were working on today."

"I didn't know you cared about cartography, Eleanor."

"I don't. I care about power and how it is exercised."

"Whose power?"

"Mine."

"What an interesting thought, that you have power."

Eleanor laughed. She had caught the gibe, but it had not hit home. So she did have something over him after all.

"All right, my dear, what are you proposing? What great alliance serves your scheme for power?"

"I want control, Paul. Total control. I choose the targets. You implement my orders."

"So my contribution is to be strength. What could you possibly offer to match it?"

"Silence, my sweet."

"Silence?"

"Yes. Silence."

"About what, Eleanor?"

"To begin with, your plot to overthrow Diana."

"What plot?"

"Second, your sabotage of the fifth column."

"What an interesting idea."

"And third, your participation in the fifth column."

"Your accusations suggest I'm a very busy man. Counter-counter espionage I think they call it. Dangerous business. One never knows whom to trust. What makes you think I would trust you?"

"You need me."

"You think so."

"I know so."

"I had never suspected it. So you must instruct me, Eleanor. How do I need you? What could I possibly need from you?"

Eleanor started to laugh. She moved toward him again, pressed her body to his, and looked up at him. There was no submission in her look, though she placed herself below him so that he could feel his own dominance just in looking down at her.

"You need me to synthesize these." She held up the capsule that held his supply of resistance antitoxin. *So that's what she was hunting for.* "You need me to synthesize these for personal use only. The Bates laboratory could then be destroyed. The fifth-column efforts in the temperate zones would be eliminated. And your control of half of Earth would be complete."

Paul considered the plan she outlined. He had not considered destroying Scientific Frontiers. That was Diana's key to power. He looked down at the science officer whose body offered bed and whose mind offered trap.

"I'll think about it."

"I don't doubt that at all."

"Now, get dressed and get out of here. I have work to do."

Shock and anger registered on Eleanor's face. She had not expected his rejection. She recovered quickly. She turned the capsule in front of her and then palmed it. He was tempted to wrestle it away from her, but that would reduce the struggle to a petty physical battle. She was correct. He could use her talents, at least the ones in the laboratory. He let her keep the capsule and watched as she dropped the robe to the floor at his feet and then stepped back and walked with dignity to the chair where her uniform lay.

She dressed as seductively as many women undress, carefully, without awkward tugs or loss of balance. Each garment moved into place on her body as if choreographed to cover her while increasing her allure.

Fully dressed, she assumed the aloofness that she had always had with him in the past.

"Perhaps when you've eliminated the priest we can talk again."

"Perhaps, Eleanor."

The door slid open as she approached it and closed automatically behind her.

He reprogrammed the code to the one Patricia would use and reset the video monitor to preprogrammed images, his "Do Not Disturb" sign for the ship at large.

He stretched out on the bed to wait.

Eliminated the priest. There it was again, the challenge and the resistance to it. He tried to figure out why he was so reluctant to carry out the order. He had met the young man before they had come to Earth. There was nothing special about him. Paul hadn't particularly liked him. He seemed aloof, too sure of himself, too obedient to The Leader. And yet each time the issue had come up over the last weeks, he had avoided it. He had let Jeffrey chase him, but he had hoped Jeffrey would fail. Had he merely wanted the privilege himself? And if he had, why had he avoided the pursuit? Now he had no choice. He was responsible for the death of Hadad. Responsible directly to Diana.

Patricia opened the door, checked the passageway again as she entered, crossed to him as the door closed behind her. She had expected him to be out of uniform, and as she crossed the room, she had reached up to undo her own uniform and join him in bed. When she noticed that he was dressed, she refastened the uniform and stood beside him, waiting.

"You weren't wrong. But plans have changed."

"I understand, sir."

"Perhaps better than I do. Diana expects the priest to be killed."

"Yes, sir."

"I want the information from him about the resistance here before he is dispatched."

"Yes, sir."

"Does that seem inconsistent to you?"

"Yes, sir."

"Patricia, I need the fifth-column support in this. The development of the antitoxin will open the northern states to the entire fleet. The resistance here must be strengthened. I can be of no assistance without the position I hold. If I do not fulfill Diana's orders to eliminate the priest, I will lose my command."

"I understand, sir."

"The priest and the girl . . . are they alone in the mountains?"

"Yes, sir. As far as we can tell, sir, the other cabins there are deserted."

"Then a large force is not necessary."

"That's true, sir."

"Good. We will take three craft. You and Jeffrey and I will take the lead. Make sure Justine includes all the personnel that Jeffrey has commandeered in this little rebellion of his. And the rest of the crew should all be of the fifth column."

"Sir?"

"I don't want to have to explain myself to anyone. Jeffrey and those he has influenced must be eliminated. He is an irritant; I can do better without him. We will stage an attack. It is important that in the first interchange of fire Jeffrey and his followers die. If there are only fifth columnists with us, there will be no witnesses."

"I see, sir."

"We will question the priest. We must know what bases the fifth column has in the northern states. We must know how he anticipated the purge, how he escaped the V-dust. His tactics and alliances will help us. Patricia, we must defeat Diana. Anything he can tell us about the resistance will be of benefit."

"I understand, sir."

"Inform Justine. We will wait the seventy-two hours until the appropriate people can return to the planet. Advise her that no one is to shoot the priest until I give the order."

"Yes, sir."

"And he must be killed. Let that be understood."

"If you say so, sir."

"And, Patricia."

"Yes, sir?"

"Eleanor just left with my supply of resistance antitoxin. Get it back for me. Without her knowing who took it."

"Yes, sir."

Patricia left his quarters. He was tired, but he had one more person to see before he could sleep.

He went to the console, reset all the controls again,

and summoned communications.

"Yes, sir."

"Have Jeffrey meet me in the chart room."

"Yes, sir."

The chart room was the most brightly illuminated space aboard the ship. Large screens covered every inch of the six walls, and the conference table itself was illuminated, itself a screen on which maps could be placed for consideration and delineation of strategies. The walls and table were brilliantly white at the moment, no pictures or maps augmented the decor. Paul had no need of maps. He had selected the room for the meeting because of the absolute inviolable privacy it afforded.

Jeffrey stood at the far end of the long table as Paul came into the room.

"You wanted to see me, Paul?"

"I did. I do."

"Concerning?"

"My conditions for your participation in the elimination of Hadad."

"I'm listening."

"You will speak to no one about the mission. Is that understood? Only you and I will know the exact timing of this endeavor."

"If you insist."

"I do. And that includes Eleanor."

"Of course."

"You will ride with me and my pilot. I have no interest in having you at my back."

"A reasonable precaution."

"The duty officer will assign the crew without your interference."

"Should I have reason to interfere?"

"We will leave in seventy-two hours."

"There is no reason for that long a delay."

"There is one reason for that delay, Jeffrey. One

and only one reason. I choose it."

There was a moment when Paul was not certain in which direction Jeffrey would turn. He had undermined Paul's authority in other ways before. But something indefinable was already beaten in Jeffrey. Paul sensed it, and so without further consideration he turned his back on his opponent and walked from the room.

Chapter 18

The sun was warm on the water in the large tub. Hadad sat watching Ruth as she splashed the warmed water around her. She smiled. He had not seen her smile, it seemed, for days.

They had found the cabins easily. And as Ruth had predicted, they were empty. Locks secured the doors except one. There they had found rooms stripped bare of all but pieces too heavy to move.

The frame of a large bed filled a second room. A flat board remained that had cradled the mattress that was gone. Heavy curtains hung at the windows, faint reminders of modesty and privacy that had been important to the former customers of the mountain spa.

Ruth had played with the switches in each room, but no lights responded. Water ran from the faucets and the toilet flushed, but those were the last vestiges of technological sophistication.

Above the cabin they had found open was a large two-story wooden building. The doors were locked, but through the windows they could see tables in one room, couches and chairs in another. Behind the lodge were four large tubs, and water remained in them though branches floated on the surfaces.

Hadad and Ruth had picked the branches and leaves from the water in one of the tubs and then hastily put aside clothes and climbed into the naturally heated water.

Ruth splashed the water up around her and laughed as it sprinkled down on her head.

Water rippled through the riverbed, a constant murmur. A bird's staccato echoed Ruth's laugh.

She moved to him across the large hot tub, her body submerged, and reached up with wet fingers to touch his lips. She looked first at his face, then into his eyes.

"I wish I could see your real eyes."

"Are you sure? You know what happened the last time," he teased her.

"Yes, I'm sure." She lay back on the water, farther away, still watching him.

Hadad pulled back the heavy lids and took the lenses from his eyes. He held them carefully in his left hand.

She turned over in the water and moved closer to him again, bringing her face close to his, searching as she looked at him.

"It must hurt you to keep them in all the time."

"It is not comfortable. But I have gotten used to it."

"Your eyes change color."

"Yes."

"What makes them change?"

"The way I feel. The thoughts I have."

"Then, if I learned the colors, I would know what you were thinking."

"Perhaps. Yours change, too, but not the color."

"And do you know what I am thinking?"

"Sometimes."

The intensity of her look changed, and Hadad felt the pull toward her again.

"That thought I know."

"Do you?"

He leaned forward and kissed her.

"Yes."

She smiled and lay back again in the water.

Gradually she floated almost to the surface and the smooth arch of her body lay suspended without tension.

Hadad closed his eyes against the daylight. His lids were sore from the lenses, sore from fatigue, sore from the smoke of the day before, from the sand in the lake water, sore from squinting against the now brighter daylight that his own eyes were unaccustomed to.

He was tired, and the concerns of the day were not behind him.

"Ruth." He spoke her name, but she did not respond.

He opened his eyes and reached out to tap her arm as it floated in front of him.

"Hmmm?" She raised her head, and her body came upright in the water.

"If we are to stay here, we must do things to make it possible."

"It's so relaxing here in the water."

"It is too relaxing. I will fall asleep soon, and you will go hungry."

"That would never do."

"I do not know how to find the grasses you eat."

"I will eat as you do."

Hadad shook his head and smiled.

"I cannot imagine that. I will find you meat. But I do not expect you to eat as I eat."

"Well . . . maybe not exactly as you eat." Ruth smiled. "All right, taskmaster. To work. To work."

She got out of the water and shook her hair free of the water, spraying Hadad and the pile of clothes beside the tub. With her hands she brushed the lingering water from her body, and then she dressed, pulling the leather clothes tight to her body to hold in the warmth it retained from the water.

Hadad dressed quickly, guarding the lenses he still held in his hand.

They walked back to the cabin. The air inside was cool and the rooms were musty. The car was parked in front of the cabin toward the road. Hadad would need a way to carry back animals for Ruth. He went to the car and looked among the items thrown into the backseat.

"We might as well bring it all in." Ruth was right behind him. "What you aren't looking for, I'll use somehow."

They gathered up the loose bundles and carried them into the house.

There was a little container that held grommets among the tools. Hadad dumped the metal findings on the counter and put the lenses from his left hand into the small metal box. He left the box there on the counter as well and went back to the car to help Ruth with the rest.

The piles of familiar items made the room more welcoming. Hadad watched Ruth as she looked around, this time seeing not the sparseness of the barren walls, but the possibilities they held. He smiled. He had seen the look before, when they had cleared the ground for the tent. Then he had not known the thoughts, the images that lay behind the quick darting calculations of the eyes. Now he understood, and welcomed the understanding.

He took the satchel, dumped its contents on the floor, and left to find food.

Crickets and beetles whetted his appetite. He caught two squirrels, ate one, and hit the other one against a rock so that he could bring it back to Ruth. A bird eluded him. A lizard did not. The sweet meat was a welcome treat. He found three brown mice, ate one, twisted the necks of the other two, and put them into the bag.

He found a hill of black ants, dug them out, and ate them by the handfuls. He thought of taking some back for Ruth, but could not figure out a way to contain them. It would not do to have them crawling in the fur of the squirrel, for that he would cut away.

He had headed back when he almost stepped on the snake that lay on the path soaking up the last rays of the afternoon sun. He caught it, bit off the head, and coiled the length of its body so it would fit into the bag.

He gathered trillium, blackberry, mountain balm, and rosemary to freshen the air in the cabin, and miner's lettuce for the flowers on top to brighten the room. The purple flower on the wild chives caught his attention, and so he grabbed a handful of the flowers and leaves.

She had dug a pit and started a fire in it behind the cabin. Chips of wood glowed brightly and branches laid above them blazed as the needles and leaves still attached dried and burned off. A large flat stone lay in the middle of the glowing coals.

The hatchet and a knife lay beside the fire.

He laid the herbs to the side and took the squirrel from the bag. With the hatchet he removed the head and cut the skin away from the muscles of the body.

Ruth came out with a can she had found and filled with water. She placed it on one side of the flat rock. She watched as he tore at the flesh.

"Here, let me do that."

Practiced hands took the knife and cut away the skin, cut the abdomen and pulled away the intestines, threw them into the forest.

"You are throwing away the best part."

She smiled up at him, then cut the animal into quarters and lay the pink meat on the rock beside the can of water.

She looked into the bag and found the mice and snake. He waited for her reaction and was surprised that she did not wince or hesitate. As deftly, she slit the skin of the snake and, taking hold of the loose skin, turned it inside out, leaving the naked meat in one long strip. She cut it into pieces and took a stick which she had obviously prepared while he was gone and speared them.

The mice she looked at, turned over in her hands, and looked at again. At last she took the knife, cut each head off, threw the heads out into the forest, and peeled the fur away from the pink flesh beneath. She worked tediously over each little piece. Hadad decided that in the future he would eat the mice himself, bring back the larger animals. When she had trimmed the mice to her satisfaction, she speared them on the stick as well and rested the stick over the fire; the two tails dangled above the flames and in time caught fire and burned away.

With another stick she scraped the squirrel off the rock and turned it over.

Hadad reached for the herbs to take them to the house.

"Where are you going with those?"

"They are for the cabin."

"They are for my dinner. Give them back."

She took some of the chive and rosemary, cut them into fine slivers, and sprinkled them over the cooking squirrel meat, put aside the rest, cut the mountain balm, trillium, and blackberry leaves and tossed them into the water, cut the flowers away from the miner's lettuce and tore the leaves from the stem that thrust up through the middle of each and put them in a pile. The purple flowers of the chives she handed back to him.

"You may have the rest," she said, looking up at him.

He looked at the few remaining leaves, the small bunch of flowers in his hand. They would have to do. He went into the cabin.

The curtains no longer hung from the windows. Boughs from the trees outside were stripped of their long needles and one curtain held them against the board frame of the bed. The other curtain covered it as a blanket. Torn bits of clothing hung as towels in the bathroom, and leather garments lay folded neatly for future use. The wood smelled wet where she had scrubbed, and fresh where she had laid pine boughs along the edges of the room. He rubbed the herbs in his hands and sprinkled them over the branches. He placed the purple flowers on the wooden table that sat against the wall. They did not match the neatness of the room. And so he took the eight blossoms and arranged them in a circle, the stems pointing toward the center, the blossoms toward the room. That was better but not right. He picked up one of the blossoms, closed the circle of seven, and tried to find a way to make the flower stand alone in the center. It would not. And to his eye the center of stems demanded the color from the flowers themselves. And so, one by one, he took the tiny petals and plucked them from the stem and placed them in a tiny circle inside the cluster of green.

He went back outside and watched her eating the cooked meats wrapped in leaves of lettuce. He sat beside her and stared into the fire.

The herbs bubbling in the water became pungent, the smoke from the fire sharp and biting.

She finished eating, then, holding the hot can with pliers that before had only worked needles through leather, poured a bit of the boiling herbed water over the rocks and knife she had used, and then put the can on the rock beside her.

Hadad watched her without comment. Carefully she sipped at the tea she had brewed.

The sky faded to gray and then to black. Stars appeared as his eyes adjusted to the lessening light. Crickets chorused and frogs added a syncopation of their own.

All day they had lived in the harsh shadows of

death. Alone now, night brought them reminders of life.

He touched her shoulder and she reached up and put her hand on top of his. And that was all that passed between them for over an hour.

The fire consumed itself and slowly faded to white ash. The evening was cool, but not cold, and they sat in the gathering darkness without need for anything more around them or between them.

"Come to bed."

She said the words not long after his eyes had closed.

He felt her get up and then take his hand to pull him to his feet. He looked up at her, but darkness absorbed her features. He got up and followed her back into the cabin.

He took the clothes from his body again. His body was weary. The curtains were smooth over the soft boughs and he collapsed into the bed, ready for sleep.

She lay beside him, and as she had before, curled close to his body, and put her head on his shoulder.

He had not expected her closeness. Except for his hands, she had not touched the lizard skin of his body, always she had stroked the torn places where the plastic human flesh still clung in patches. He had accepted that she was not upset to look at his different skin. But he had not expected for her to enfold him as she had before. He held her to him, and though there was no distance between them that could be measured, she moved closer still.

He slept.

"My son." The voice called him from across all time. He knew the voice and did not know how to answer. And so he said nothing.

Still he slept.

"Arise, my child, for the time has come." The summons had no demand, but the response of

Hadad's being was complete.

He woke without weariness, without concern for the night to come or the days past. Ruth turned in her sleep and moved away from his body as she always did. His eyes opened on the closeness of the room.

"Come." The voice continued to call to him, though his eyes were open now to the cabin and the forest around it.

He walked back through the cabin, out onto the steps, and sat naked, looking out upon the stillness of the world.

"Good." The voice spoke from a distance. Hadad waited.

Before him on the path appeared a shape in light and shadow. If the moon had been high, the figure would have been lighted by moonlight, but there was no moon. The radiance came from within it, and the shadows were of it, not on it.

"You have come down a long path, my son." The voice came from the figure, but it filled space as though it came from across a galaxy.

"I have traveled the path from the stars."

"The people of the stars shall return to the stars."

"And they that recognize the light shall not see death."

"You have remembered well."

"I do not know what I have remembered. I did not know I knew those words or why I spoke them."

"It is enough that you spoke them."

"Who are you?"

The shadowy figure remained on the walkway before him.

"You have known me before. My name is Amon. I am the last of the priests of Zon. Once we were many. Once we spoke freely of the Lords of Light. Once we opposed the ways of The Leader. Once we taught the children bearing the mark of Zon. You have learned these words from me in the house of the Elders. These words and others of the book of Zon."

"Teach me again, Amon, for I have forgotten the words."

"My son, the words are not important except for those who do not walk in the truth of Zon. For them the words disrupt, confuse, challenge, and destroy. For those who know the truth they comfort, clarify, support, and enlighten. But for those who walk in the path of Zon, they do not matter."

"But I have forgotten the teachings of Zon. In my head are only the words of The Leader, the words of Diana."

"The words you speak of are only in your mind. The teachings of Zon fill your being. Zon teaches compassion for others, and your being speaks of compassion for others. Zon teaches compliance with the laws of the universe, and your being moves in harmony with all that is. Zon teaches acceptance of the balance of all actions, and your being walks without wonder the narrow margin between life and death. Zon teaches worthiness in all things, and your being has acknowledged the worthiness of all that was not you. From Ruth you are learning the worthiness of all that is you. This is all you need to know."

"But you have come here. Why have you come now if not to teach me?"

"The time has come for the Lords of Light to redeem the Earth. Listen carefully, for there is much to do:

"In three days you will leave this place and fly south to find Elizabeth."

"Elizabeth?"

"She is called the Star Child. You will recognize her, for she carries the mark of Zon.

"The followers of Zon will call you Amon, for they will see in you what they expect of me, and the book of Zon teaches that one named Amon will take the people back to the stars. People have asked your name, and you have given to each something that they could say with comfort and with ease. You have chosen each name for a purpose. Now the name of Amon chooses you for a purpose. The followers of Zon will recognize in you the power of the Lords of Light. And you may call them friends, for they will know the truth of you. And all whom they call friends will assist you, for you walk in the light. And they shall not experience death on this planet, for having seen the light in you, they, too, shall walk in light.

"The child, Elizabeth, will go with you wherever you lead, for she has been forewarned that Amon will come to her. And you will learn as she has learned to use the powers of Zon to witness to that power in the Earth. Strike down only those who would do you harm. But know that you can call upon the waters on the Earth and above the Earth to do your bidding, and that the substance of the Earth itself and all that lives upon it will respond to your word.

"You will teach Elizabeth the ways of Zon, for she does not understand the power that works through her. And you will travel with her for three and half years, bringing the ways of Zon to all the peoples of Earth before the two of you will experience death.

"And for each of those years you walk in the light of the Lords of Light, you will experience one day of separation from the light. But then you shall stand again, though you were dead, and thereafter you shall be able to walk among the stars as I do.

"The child Ruth bears will die to fulfill the prophecy of the books of Earth. But the child she will carry of your seed will be strong and prosper on the Earth and shall do battle for the preservation of the people of Earth. And the followers of Zon will watch over Ruth when you depart. For she must fulfill her heritage and embrace your people as her people.

"Now return to your sleep, my child. And be not troubled, for all that I have told you has been foreseen among both peoples. Repeat the covenant, my son."

"Zon is the cause for which I would die, but there is no cause for which I would kill."

"For in Zon there is no death, but only the light of love."

The figure spoke the covenant response and then disappeared from the path.

Hadad sat in the quiet of the night. An owl called from a nearby tree, and wild hyssop filled the air with sweetness.

He was not certain how long Ruth had stood behind him before he noticed her presence. He reached behind him and pulled her legs to his back. She touched his head with her fingers, but said nothing to break the stillness.

He felt her skin begin to cool, and so he stood and put his arm around her and led her back to bed.

There in the soft folds, in the warmth still held in the fabric from her body, he held her to him and knew the touch of her body with his body, knew the look of her eyes with his eyes, and melded with all of her being with all that he was and ever would be.

In the morning there was only the morning. Afternoon brought only the afternoon, and twilight only twilight. Nothing disturbed the passage of the sun.

Hadad walked through the woods. The high forest was different from the lumbered orderly ridges of Vida. Aspen, pine, fir, and cedar battled for light, and meadow grasses and shrubs blanketed the contours of the land. He followed the river. The running water was cold, apparently fed by the ice fields high above them on the peaks. But below the lodge were natural pools of incredibly hot water. He looked for the source of one of the pools and found it beneath a rock about three feet high buried in the side of a steep bank.

The water smelled of minerals. Hadad tasted it and found it salty.

He climbed the steep bank and found flat prairies edged with cedar and fir, and more pools of hot water. He skirted the pools and wandered the woods beyond the lower prairie, climbing as the hillside rose into the trees. Another pool emerged in the shadows of trees, and there stood a deer.

She watched him as he approached. And satisfied that he came not as man, not as hunter, not as predator, the doe continued to lick at the salted water. He squatted beside the pool and watched. He was observed as well. He felt eyes from the forest watching. And when he did not move, did not change the forest stillness, an elk, old, with a heavy rack, came and stood beside him at the spring.

The day was long enough to hold the waiting, the watching, the lingering.

When the elk and deer had gone, he returned to the river. He crossed the footbridge and found other pools dotting a meadow on the other side.

A skunk crossed his path, rabbits darted through the tall grass. A hawk circled high above him.

The bear saw him before he recognized that the shadow against the forest was alive. He had not seen a bear before. And so he watched and followed, keeping the distance even between them.

The bear ignored him, stopped for berries, explored the springs in the meadow, stretched his back against a tree to scratch, dug in the forest for insects. But when the bear had had enough of his constant companionship, he turned and growled.

It might have been enough to stop and turn to go, but Hadad climbed. The tree was there beside him, and he found himself high in the branches. He was not pursued. The bear assessed his position, and then disappeared into the forest.

Hadad waited. And then he returned to the cabin.

By the third day Hadad began to trust the quiet rhythms of the mountains undisturbed by the life-and-death dramas of man. He hunted, and took only the food that was willing to be eaten. Ruth had gone with him the second day, and though she did not have the reflexes to take food with her hand, he found that she could stop a bird in flight with the knife she carried between her shoulders.

She did not flinch when he ate food that was still alive, and he learned to gather berries without getting caught on the spines that protected their branches.

In the afternoons they lay in the warm water of the large tub and she teased him about the patches of pink that he wore on his feet and that still grew to him on parts of his back and about his head and neck. The scratches healed and gradually the surfaces began to grow back over his legs, down over his shoulders.

"How can it do that?" she asked as she examined the new tender places over his collarbone.

"It grows."

"But you call it plastic."

"That is just my word. It is what you call symbiote."

"You mean symbiotic?"

"Yes. It is a life form. It grows to cover me. It eats from my skin. I keep it alive. And it keeps me alive."

"But do you have to have it on you?"

"No. I did not have it before I was on the ship."

"Can it grow without you?"

"No. Without a host it will die. But on my planet there are many hosts. Here there are none but us."

"Oh. Then there are two invaders of Earth."

Hadad laughed. "You could say that."

"I just did."

They dressed to hunt. The day was warm, but the bushes were sharp and so they wore the leathers that would best protect them.

Something disturbed the air. Hadad listened and tried to distinguish what it was, but the sound stopped and did not begin again. He finished fastening the sleeves of his shirt and watched Ruth run her fingers through her hair and shake it out behind her. She pulled the strands back and wrapped them around her hand and took a long leatherworking needle and wove it through the strands, holding the knot of hair up off her neck.

Hadad put his fingers on the back of her neck. She was warm, his fingers soon took the heat, releasing some of their coolness to her skin.

She turned and faced him, the eyes of the deer begging him to come closer.

"This morning we will hunt. Come."

She wrinkled her nose and smiled and was the first to the door despite his urgency.

She opened the door, saw the weapon in the hand of the uniformed lizard, and threw the knife to pin his arm against the tree behind him before he could fire. And so it was the weapon of the small female Visitor behind him that fired at the roof above her head. And only Hadad's hand on her shoulder stopped Ruth's forward motion before the body of the male Visitor from the roof landed on the steps in front of the door.

Hadad recognized the fallen lizard as Jeffrey and watched as the life left him.

There were four other shots: two beside the bedroom window, another behind the cabin, one felling the uniformed male who was running up the path toward the door. And then the firing stopped.

"This is my battle, Ruth. They have found me. They want me, not you." He took her in his arms and kissed her and then moved past her to the doorway.

He stepped over the body of Jeffrey as he descended the steps.

"Amon." The Visitor still pinned to the tree whispered the name.

Hadad looked up and recognized the officer as one whom he had known at The Leader's compound on the planet he called home.

"The people of the stars shall return to the stars." Paul recited the ritual words.

"And they that recognize the light shall not see death." Hadad completed the response.

"Amon. You have come to Earth. It is the time of the returning."

"It is the beginning. You have come to kill me."

"No. We have come to ask about the resistance."

"There is no resistance. There is only balance in the actions of all things."

"The teachings of Zon."

"You know them?"

Paul looked away from him for the first time, glancing over his shoulder at the uniformed Visitors around him. Hadad looked at each of them. There was no recognition in their eyes. Only in the eyes of Paul. And then he knew the cause of Paul's distress. He did not understand why the others did not fire on him or rush to bind him. He waited for the answer.

"Yes. I know the teachings of Zon."

"Then you are my friend. And if these are your friends, I accept them as my own."

"Sir?" The small woman behind Paul spoke.

"Yes, Patricia."

"If there is no resistance, that would explain the operations."

"Yes. Yes, it would."

"And it would mean that . . . that he is not part of the fifth column."

"Patricia, that is true. But that is not the resistance he is talking about."

"I do not understand, sir."

"Learn now the ways of Zon. This is not a priest of The Leader. This is Amon, the priest of Zon, who will release the people of Earth and return us to the stars." He stroked her hair with his free arm, and then for the first time seemed to realize he could not move the other.

Hadad stepped forward to the tree and removed Ruth's knife from Paul's sleeve.

Patricia looked at Paul questioningly, and then she looked at Hadad and shook her head from side to side, her expression full of wonder.

"I *was* the man you looked for." Hadad tried to address the questions she had asked before, to give some orientation, some guidance, something familiar for the girl to relate to. But she just continued to shake her head from side to side and watch his face.

The rhythm of the movement was hypnotic, and for a few moments Hadad saw only the girl. Then he became aware of the four others who stood now to his right: a woman and three men stood with weapons pointed at him, but with no intention to fire.

Nothing in the prophecy he had heard in the night gave him any notion of what he was to do next. He stood in the middle of the path and looked back at Paul, who seemed to be the leader of the expedition. He waited for some clue as to the goal of their mission. He sensed that they had come to kill him, but that they suddenly could not. And it was suddenly very confusing to them all, for nothing at all seemed to be happening.

No one knew what to do, and no action outside of them demanded a familiar response.

They needed a plan. And Hadad was a leader, so he

started creating order within the confusion he faced.

"Paul, Ruth and I are to find the Star Child, Elizabeth. You will come with us. We will need a pilot and a craft. The rest will return to the ship and report that the priest you sought has been eliminated; he is no more. That should satisfy Diana."

"Justine," Paul echoed Hadad's authority. "Take the rest of the crew back to the ship. Patricia will go with us. Report the craft we take as destroyed. I'm sure you can invent ground forces sufficient to explain the casualties."

"Yes, sir. That will not be difficult."

"Remember what you have seen here, but speak of it to no one."

"I understand, sir."

"Dismissed."

The crew of four departed.

"Your craft is not close by."

"No, we did not want to risk your escape into the forest."

"Bring it here."

"Yes, sir." Paul and the pilot he called Patricia ran up the road in the direction the others had taken.

Hadad returned to the cabin. He climbed the steps, over the body of the man who had been his guardian and his nemesis for so many years. He squatted on the top stair, beside the face contorted in death, broken by the edge of the step where it had landed.

"Praetenama, Jeffrey. Praetenama."

He put his hand on the forehead of his friend and stood up, turning to find Ruth inside the door.

He handed her the throwing knife he had taken from the tree.

"What's happening, Hadad? I don't understand."

"I do not know either. All I do know is that we have to find the Star Child, Elizabeth."

"Can't we stay here, just the two of us, together?"

He reached across to her and kissed her, and then he smiled. The hover craft landed on the road behind the car.

"I would like that too, Ruth. I am not a warrior. I do not like to walk amid the violence. But there is balance in the actions of all things. And while the Earth is at war, there is no peace. We could not save Prineville, nor the people of Vida or Detroit, but perhaps we *can* do something for what remains of the world."